The Nocturnals

Also from Metaphorosis

<u>Verdage</u>

Reading 5X5 x2: Duets
Score – an SFF symphony
Reading 5X5: Readers' Edition
Reading 5X5: Writers' Edition

<u>Metaphorosis Magazine</u>

Metaphorosis: Best of 20xx
Metaphorosis 20xx: The Complete Stories
annual issues, from 2016

Monthly issues

<u>Plant Based Press</u>

Best Vegan Science Fiction & Fantasy
annual issues, from 2016

from B. Morris Allen:
Chambers of the Heart: speculative stories
Susurrus
Allenthology: Volume I
Tocsin: and other stories
Start with Stones: collected stories
Metaphorosis: a collection of stories

The Nocturnals

by

Mariah Montoya

ISBN: 978-1-64076-072-1 (e-book)
ISBN: 978-1-64076-078-3 (paperback)
ISBN: 978-1-64076-079-0 (hardcover)

from
Metaphorosis Publishing

Neskowin

Contents

Evening

Damien had discovered the marsh after their last Move.

A portion of his school's portable fence had been damaged during the long trek from west to east: during recess, he and his friends could now wiggle between crooked wires and flump onto the soil beyond the playground turf. Mrs. Zemukil never noticed them sneak away. She was usually yelling at Timby Jenkins for some shenanigan or the other. Right now, Timby was near the shiny new playset, selling cups of his own color-dyed piss to classmates.

Mrs. Zemukil's shrieks faded as Damien and his friends crept through the weeds around the school's storage shed, giggling. The great marsh glimmered behind it, oozing with promise: it was here they always found all sorts of new bugs and spiders squirming beneath the mud.

"Okay, we've only got half an arcsec!" Damien told his friends when they reached the edge. They thudded to their hands and knees. Mud spattered their pants, but that was okay; last time Mrs. Zemukil had asked where all the filth came from, Timby Jenkins had asked her where all *her* filth came from, and Mrs. Zemukil had been quiet about the mud ever since. Damien didn't like Timby Jenkins and his pranks much, but bless that boy's heart for saving him and his friends from recess ban. "Whoever finds the biggest one gets to have everyone else's cookie at lunch!" he added, because when sweets were the motivation, they usually found a monster.

The boys all got to work, punching fists through the mud in their search for alien critters. Damien glanced at the sun lodged low in the eastern sky. It was, the clocks read, about twelve degrees from the horizon. Mom said they'd have to Move again soon, when the sun sank two degrees lower and the bells started clanging, but he would be sad to leave the marsh behind. They'd been learning about the planet's rotation in school; if only the aro spun the other way—if only the sun rose in the east and set in the west like it did for other planets—the days and nights wouldn't last so long. They might be able to survive the night, to Stay, and he'd be able to play at the marsh's edge forever.

But as it was, the night was endlessly dangerous. The night would kill them.

He slid his fingers beneath a thick carpet of moss, trying to locate anything other than slimy sludge. Nothing. The marsh smelled like spoiled eggs, and the same old gnats hovered above its surface. The clattering sound of his classmates playing and screaming wafted over the storage shed, and the sun's lingering warmth bathed his back. The boy kept digging, found a few familiar flopping worms. Then, after a quarter arcsec had passed, he felt a sharp pinch on his fingertip. He withdrew a hand dripping with muck and blood.

"Hey, check it out!" he hollered.

His friends came sloshing over. He showed them his finger, and soon they were all tunneling with sticks and rocks until they excavated the beast: a caterpillar-like beetle with pincers lining its back and a single, bulging yellow eye. As they passed it from palm to muddy palm, the beetle's pincers clamped furiously. Its eyeball began oozing a sour green pus.

"Cool!"

"It looks like a deformed penis."

"Let *me* hold it!"

Damien opened his mouth to announce what he was going to name his discovery, but his mouth stayed hinged open. No sound came out. The creature fell between his fingertips and squirmed back into the mud.

His skin tingled. Goosebumps frosted his neck.

I'm having a reaction to the bite, Damien managed to think, staring wide-eyed at his friends. In the distance, the school chimes clamored. Half an arcsec had passed, but he couldn't move. The tingles scuttled up his body.

"Damien, we've got to go," he heard dimly. Slimed hands clamped around his wrists, tugging him away from the marsh. But the tingles were telling him something now, planting words into his head—not like a voice, but like thoughts, like he was talking to himself.

Go west, where the sun rises every sixty years. We need you in the west, Damien. It will not be scary. You will only be going back the way you and your community came.

His friends were shouting now, shaking his shoulders, but the boy merely repeated it to himself, tasting truth in the words:

I'll go west, where the sun rises every sixty years. They need me in the west. It will not be scary. I'll only be going back to where I came from. The tingles cocooned him, swaddling him in armor made of goosebumps and strange, brilliant new ideas.

I'll go west, where the sun rises. They need me. Not scary. I'll be going back.

Ignoring his friends, the boy shook off their grips and drifted toward the marsh. Going west would be easy. He wouldn't have to squint at the sun. He was headed toward the purple part of sky, where darkness crouched and would welcome him with twilight arms. And *they* were there, the creatures who wanted to tell him something.

Something important.

"Damien!" his friends wailed behind him.

He felt himself trudge toward the bank, his shoes squelching and sinking deep into mud. He threw himself into the marsh, where he treaded thick water, leech-like plants clinging to his skin. There were many things beneath the mottled green surface, bugs he and his friends hadn't dared to discover. He felt them bite his legs and fasten onto his arms, but the pinpricks were only an echo of pain, as if they were happening to someone else, not him.

When Damien finally kicked and clawed his way to the other end of the marsh and crawled up the bank, his body was covered in sucker slugs that had attached themselves to his neck and blood fish that dangled from his elbows.

West. Sun rises. Need me. Scary. Going back.

His friends' shouts were distant now. The school chimes had stopped. Damien left the marsh and his classmates behind, stumbling toward the foothills beyond the community limits, where swaying grass rose high above his head. He barreled into the grasses, away from the sun, toward the darkness that whispered his name.

"Damien Fertheli. Ten years old."

Joah Cadshaw read his notes as he weaved between vendors and whisked down an unnamed dirt street between trailer houses. "Mother: Lupita Fertheli. Father: N/A. Trailer Three-Five-One in the Dirt Slums. Three-Five-One, c'mon, where are you?"

Joah hated the goddamned road developers. They never assigned street names for the smallest trailers at the end of a Move. No, the poor could just clump together in one big marked territory and bicker about which pot to piss in. Joah had been summoned to break up a fight more often than the ice moon rose and fell in the sky.

The trailer numbers weren't in order, either. Joah passed numbers five, four-fifteen, sixty-three... People sat on their portable wood steps watching him through the holes in their sunhats. A few children raced down the rows, hitting an old aluminum can with crooked sticks. One of the kids was naked. A nasty rash had turned his left butt cheek into a bloodberry patch.

"You need something, Mister?" a voice rasped.

Joah looked up, but didn't locate the source of the noise until an old woman banged a saucepan against her wood window-frame. The woman's wrinkled face poked between two flaps of blanket nailed to the outside of her trailer.

"Yes, actually." The sun was half-concealed behind her house, but even at twelve degrees, it still made him squint. When they'd finally stopped Moving to set up camp here a little more than a year ago, it had been at a twenty-two-degree angle in the sky: fierce and hot and blinding. Joah had always shuddered to imagine ninety degrees, when the sun would blaze directly overhead. "Do you know where Lupita Fertheli lives?" he asked the woman. "Her son, Damien, went missing about seven moon cycles ago."

"Ah, yes, Lupita." The woman jabbed a thumb to her left. "Just keep walking till you get to the trailer surrounded by rocks—Jarold Hansen likes to mark his shithole with pebbles, it seems—and then make a right. Lupita's is the one with all the mud holes in front." She paused. Scratched her crinkled forehead. "Damien liked to dig."

"Thank you."

Joah strode on, trying not to catch all the eyes staring at him. When he found the mobile home surrounded by holes, he paused. Damien Fertheli had apparently liked to dig until the ground resembled cavitied cheese. Besides the demolished land, though, Lupita's house was nothing remarkable: shabby, stained white trailer, its wheels sunk in mud, sheets for curtains.

The door opened. A woman flew down the steps, her hair in frazzled knots.

"Oh, thank God you're here! Why'd it take them so long to send someone?

You're Detective Cadshaw, right? Come in, come in, please."

The woman took him by the hand and tugged him up the steps, into the dim interior of her home. Joah wiped his hands on his pants when she released him —her fingers had been gloved with cold sweat—but Lupita Fertheli didn't notice; she was too busy fussing over the fire stove, trying to pour him a cup of tea with shaky hands.

"Mrs. Fertheli, it's okay. I'm not thirsty. Please just sit down."

"Okay. Yeah, okay."

They sat at the cramped table, facing each other. Joah brushed aside some crumbs and slapped down his notes, but before he could start, Lupita spoke through a plugged nose.

"Y-you look familiar, Detective. Have I seen you before?"

"No," Joah said automatically, but he felt a chill despite the stuffiness of the trailer. This woman probably *had* seen him before. In the newspaper headlines. Or maybe she had been in the crowd lining the High Road during the incident itself. But that had been years ago, before the last Move, too long ago for strangers to remember the details.

When Lupita nodded absentmindedly, Joah cleared his throat,

whipped out his pen, and looked down at his notes.

"Okay, I have here that your son, Damien, never came inside from recess seven cycles ago. He was playing with friends off school grounds. All his friends returned to the school saying that he'd wandered off without them."

"Yes, yes." Lupita tugged at a hangnail with her teeth. Her eyes were puffy, like half-moons hiding behind swollen pink clouds. "That's what Rayna Zemukil said, anyway. I never got to talk to Damien's friends. Apparently, they were all upset and wanted to go home. But look, I know Damien wouldn't just... wander off. I—I think maybe the N—"

"Do you remember what Damien was wearing, Mrs. Fertheli?" Joah said, cutting her off.

He knew what she had been about to say. At the word *Nocturnal*, his blood always seemed to freeze beneath his skin. Parents *always* wanted to blame their runaways on the Nocturnals, but the Nocturnals only chose one victim a year, and it was never a child.

Lupita didn't respond. She stared at him wide-eyed, and Joah saw his hunched silhouette reflected in her glassy pupils. Fresh tears shined them.

"What was Damien wearing, Mrs. Fertheli?" Joah repeated gently.

"I think it was—yes, it was his green shirt with the cat on it. He always wanted a cat. He loves how wild they are, but I—I always told him no. I shouldn't have told him no."

"It's okay," Joah said. He paused. "Can you give me the names of Damien's friends?"

"Y-yes, sure. There's Pedar Montrone. Cale Lyle. Sampson—I don't remember his last name. I'm not sure Damien ever said. And then he always talked about Timby Jenkins. I don't think they were actually friends, but maybe you could interview Timby too?"

"Timby Jenkins," Joah repeated, jotting the name down in his notes. "Thank you, Mrs. Fertheli. Now, tell me— what's Damien's behavior been like lately? Has he been acting out—throwing tantrums or avoiding you? Showing any other signs of distress?"

"No." Lupita blinked up at him. She grabbed the swaying tail of the sheet hanging from her window, pressed the cloth to her nostrils, and blew.

"Can you tell me about Damien's father?" Joah said, trying to avoid looking at the crusted red bulge of her nose.

"No, I can't." Tears leaked from the swollen humps of Lupita's eyes. "I can't tell you about Damien's father because this has nothing to *do* with his father. Damien wasn't acting out. He was a happy boy. He'd never leave his friends or his school or *me*."

"Lupita," Joah started.

"*No*. Detective, I know you want to uncover some shit reason why my son ran away, but he didn't run away. I'm telling you—just like I told Rayna Zemukil—I think the... I think *they* got him." She lowered her voice to a nasal whisper. "The *Nocturnals*."

"Listen, Lupita." Goosebumps tickled Joah's neck, but it was no longer an iciness that flooded the pit of his stomach; it was heat. An old anger. "The Nocturnals have never infected anybody younger than twenty. They wouldn't have taken a child."

"Says who?" Lupita whimpered. "I'm sorry, Detective, but what if they wanted to change their... their *taste* in victims? My baby might be stumbling around in the darkness as we—"

"Your baby is not," Joah said through a carefully clenched jaw, "stumbling around in the darkness. We can *crawl* faster than the sun moves across the sky."

"Exactly. My boy could have walked to the Eternal Night by now."

"He can't have walked to the Eternal Night," Joah said, his voice rising, "because first, the Eternal Night doesn't exist—a night lasts the same as a day, thirty years. It's not eternal. Second, there's twelve degrees between us and the first signs of darkness, which means your boy would have to walk more than a thousand kilometers just to reach *sunset*. I don't know if you've ever been at zero degrees, Mrs. Fertheli, when the sun is sitting on the horizon—"

"Of course I haven't," whispered Lupita, pressing a palm against her heart.

"Imagine all those times the sun's hidden behind a tree or a hill or something, then. Even when it's sunset, there's still light outside. Sure, pink and purple light, maybe strange light, but *light*. Which means even if the Nocturnals had infected your boy, he *wouldn't have reached the darkness* by now, okay? He can't have—"

But this time, it was not Lupita Fertheli who cut Joah off. This time, the sound that crashed over them was more piercing and terrible than a grieving mother's pealing wail.

Both Joah and Mrs. Fertheli clapped hands over their ears. No, it couldn't be.

Joah checked his wristwatch. The hand hovered steadily at twelve degrees. He yelled at Lupita over the swelling noise of the bells.

"What's your clock say?"

Lupita fumbled for a timepiece behind her and thunked it onto the table.

"Twelve degrees!" she screamed.

It was too early—two degrees too early—for the Moving bells to ring. The bells were only supposed to clang across the city when the sun had reached a ten-degree angle in the sky, when the first faint signs of pink laced the clouds; they still had about ninety moon cycles until that happened. *Why* the bells were ringing now...

"Excuse me, Mrs. Fertheli."

Joah jumped up, bounded out the door, and raced down the nameless streets, pushing past streaking kids and shouting adults who had fled their trailers.

Three Moves ago, when they had set up base near an oil reserve, the warners had thrashed their bells through the open windows of moving vehicles. Now, however, the warners stampeded throughout the community on horseback, weaving between alleys with their brass bells held high above their heads.

"Pack your things!" one bellowed now, his voice hardly distinguishable over the clanging. He kicked his mare, who came trotting down the slum streets. Joah and the other onlookers stumbled back to avoid being trampled. "Check your wheels!" the warner called. "Time to Move! General Deckler's orders! Pack your things!"

When the warner, his horse, and the cacophonous bell had rounded a corner, Joah hurtled his way out of the maze-like Dirt Slums and onto the edge of the black-tarred High Road.

He could think of only one man to go to for answers, a man he hadn't spoken to since his own name had glowered on the front page of newspapers:

The leader of the community. Joah's ex-boss.

General Aoif Deckler.

"Excuse me, sir, we're not taking visitors at the moment."

Joah stopped mid-stride to look at the secretary behind the office's marble front desk—or, at least, the desk looked like marble, though it was speckled with gold. The miners must have found a new type of rock since they had settled here almost a year and a half ago. The secretary herself looked fairly new too.

"Look." Joah turned back and leaned against the marble. The secretary's cup of pens rattled as the bells continued wailing outside and footsteps stomped on the floor above their heads. "You can't have been here long. I'm Joah Cadshaw. I used to work here. For General Deckler. I was a retriever."

"I'm sorry, sir," the secretary said, with a brave quiver of her chin, "but there's only been one retriever who got relieved of duty in the last five years, and he's not allowed here."

"Yeah, I am," Joah grunted.

He turned away from the secretary's stutters, took the stairs two at a time—why Deckler insisted on *stairs* was beyond Joah; it had always made Moving a hell of a battle—and rounded the corner, to Deckler's office.

Without pausing to knock, he hurled open the door and saw Aoif Deckler, with his white sideburns and boxy build, bent over a table, talking rapidly to a female assistant. They both turned to stare at him. The assistant's eyes widened as she took in Joah's panting figure.

"Joah," Deckler said. His salt-white eyebrows raised for the tiniest second of surprise. Then, in typical Deckler style, he recovered from the shock and boomed, "Get over here, Joah, we need you! Thank

God you're here. I was *trying* to find someone to go with Crane."

"Why the *hell* are the bells ringing, Deckler?"

Joah hurried to the table, which was strewn with various maps and documents. Deckler's office was a mess. His desk had been rammed against the table to increase surface space, papers littered the carpet, and all the awards and certificates usually pinned to his wall had been crudely taken down, so that empty nails spotted the plaster. Only one poster still hung above a filing cabinet, but Joah didn't want to look at the hunched, many-eyed drawing of a Nocturnal.

"What is it, Deckler?" Joah asked, moving closer.

"Look." Deckler thrust a thick finger at the map that he and his assistant had been poring over. "The scouts came back just an arcsec ago. Brought bad fucking news. The High Road has been destroyed. Must've been a quake. There's a deep fissure in Aro's ground, about seven meters wide and two kilometers deep. Cracked the High Road in two. Maybe the retrievers' crew could cross it with the right equipment, but our whole *community*? Forget it."

Joah peered at the map, where new red ink marked the fissure the scouts had found.

The High Road, which Joah's community had been taking for decades, and which his ancestors had used the last time they had set foot on this continent, was dotted by fading black, showing the endless trek from west to east. They had been about to reach the Green Sea, a vast body of water Joah had only heard stories about, but the red ink sliced across the familiar dotted line, blocking their path.

Joah traced the fissure with his finger.

"Looks like it runs, what, five thousand kilometers north?" he asked.

Peculiarly, he didn't feel the panic that Aoif Deckler seemed to feel. An iron sense of calm had sunk deep into his stomach. Ever since he had been relieved of his retrieving duties, he'd hated how the world kept its sickly slow spin and the people around him kept their plastered smiles, as if everything were okay, despite what had happened to him.

Now here at last was proof that something was wrong.

That the world was breaking apart.

"Yes, five thousand kilometers north," Deckler said. "That's how far the scouts went, anyway, but they said the fissure kept going. And it runs about a thousand kilometers south. Then the fissure tilts southeast and finally—right here—eastward." He pointed at the curve of the red ink, which was like the graceful arc of a bowl.

Elegant, for a quake's doing, Joah thought.

Deckler massaged the bridge of his crooked nose.

"At the rate we travel as a group—twelve measly kilometers a moon cycle—we won't make it to the sea in time. We're running out of working vehicles, not to mention fuel. The horses aren't breeding fast enough. Even if we head south right now—which we're going to, that's why the bells are ringing—the sun'll go down before we make it to the end of the fissure."

Joah said nothing. *Maybe Lupita Fertheli will get to experience sunset after all*, he thought.

"We won't have time to backtrack and continue taking the High Road," Deckler continued. "We'll have to keep going east into uncharted territory. At least, we'll have to if we don't want to get swallowed by the Eternal Fucking Night."

Joah suppressed an urge to give his ex-boss the same lecture he had given Lupita.

"And then when we reach the sea," Deckler sighed, "who's to say we'll have enough time to build ships? The Nocturnals might just find themselves a *feast*. C'mon, Joah. Why aren't you saying anything? Say something or I'll lose my goddamn mind."

"Look," Joah said obediently, "we'll pick up the speed. Some people may need to abandon their things to lighten the load for the horses, or else we'll travel in waves. The first wave can go on ahead, and the horses can come back for the second wave. Sunset won't kill us. It's a few cycles *after* sunset... that's where... where *they* live. Trust me, I'd know," he added.

"I *know* you know, Joah," Deckler said. "Which is why I need you now. You working on any assignments for the law enforcement office?"

"Yeah, I'm searching for a missing kid. Never came in from recess. Why?"

"Forget the kid," Deckler said.

"What?"

Deckler glanced at his assistant, who Joah looked at properly for the first time. She was round-faced and pink with excitement. A silver pin gleamed on her uniform over her chest.

Ah, she was a recent graduate of the Retrieving Institute. Not an assistant.

"Look, Joah," Deckler said, "I'll tell your command that it's an emergency and I need you. They'll understand. Don't argue," he growled as Joah opened his mouth. "The kid'll be found during the Move, mark my words. If he's hiding in some alley, he'll come to light when the buildings around him start rolling. If somebody's got him, they won't have him for long. You can't keep a secret when you're constantly Moving. Secrets only stay secret if they're stagnant, and God knows our people can't stay stagnant. He'll be found."

"I—what do you want me to do, then?" Joah asked stiffly. Behind Deckler's blocky shoulder, the graduate was wide-eyed, leeching onto every word.

"You were the best retriever I had, Joah. Until the incident. You could find anyone within a thousand kilometers: miners who'd strayed too far, hunters trapped in a ravine, the Infected. Well, now we have *hundreds* of miners and hunters and gatherers who don't know the bells are ringing early. I've sent out all my retrievers, every single one, to go find and warn them, but I don't have enough. That's why I'm sending her—" He jerked a thumb at the graduate "— but I need someone to go with her. Someone experienced. She doesn't have a partner yet, see."

"You want me to go retrieve people again," Joah said, his stomach clenching.

"Yes. Joah, this is Misla Crane." The graduate smiled at him again, bouncing on the balls of her feet. "Misla, you're going to do everything he says, understand? I'm sending you two west. To track down the grahsm miners and oil scavengers. You remember that cylindrical tower we passed on the High Road? The one every damn man, woman, and child wanted to gawk at?"

"Yes, General," Misla Crane said eagerly.

"Good. Should be some scavengers around there searching for oil in an old reserve nearby. They left on horseback, but I'm sending *you* two in one of our last iron steeds so you can get to them within a few cycles. Should be about seven degrees where they're at, but they won't be planning to leave till five degrees." He surveyed them both with gray-eyed sharpness. "It's your two's job to tell those scavengers and miners they need to Move *right now*. You'll stick together, and you'll head back in ten cycles. Am I clear?"

Misla Crane nodded. When Deckler glared at him, Joah hesitated, grunted, and bowed his head, all too aware that he was leaving the case of Damien Fertheli behind.

"Perfect. Now get the hell out of my office," Aoif Deckler said.

The noise of the early bells dimmed as Joah and Misla Crane drove away from the city in a boxy steed, its hooded back filled with duffels of clothes, canned food, blankets, weapons, and canteens of water. They took the High Road snaking through the foothills, where bugs buzzed and the grass occasionally rustled with some kind of scurrying animal.

Nobody knew how the High Road had originated, only that it had always been there, stretching from coast to coast, constantly repaired by those who used it: Joah's people, who called themselves the Sunsetters, and the Sunrisers who migrated on the opposite side of the world and sometimes left words carved on stones to mark their passing. Occasionally, whenever they found a place to settle, they'd find squashed and crinkled cans littering the ground like community shit that wouldn't disintegrate, and they'd know the Sunrisers had found this a good spot to Stay for a couple years too.

But there were rumors of others besides them and the Sunrisers. Others besides the Nocturnals, even. Growing up, Joah had heard stories of the Leather Skins, a people who could endure the scorch of ninety degrees, who roamed freely throughout the day as they pleased, their tough skin protecting them from the sun's death rays.

Must be nice, Joah had thought as a boy, *to live in midday. You wouldn't have to Move as often.* He'd wondered why his community of Sunsetters couldn't just catch up with the Leather Skins, keep away from the dangers of night.

Joah's granddad, a retired retriever, had answered this question by dropping a purple squash in their stove and allowing it to crisp. When he'd speared the burnt squash with a poker and offered it to Joah, he had said, "You got leather skin, boy? Or would you blister?"

Joah's dreams about taking the High Road to midday had disintegrated. And now it seemed a portion of the High Road itself had disintegrated, severed by some unknown force.

"I wonder if the Nocturnals use this road," Misla Crane said now, jolting Joah from his reveries. Somewhere in the dim caverns of his mind, he realized she'd been chatting the whole time. "I wonder if they have, like, a Road Repair Crew." She laughed. "Or Traffic Control."

"Mmmm," Joah grunted.

There it was again, that word—*Nocturnals*. Better to focus on driving than let the word bind him to his old anger and the terror that simmered beneath it.

The iron steed bounced as its wheels cruised over rocks strewn across the road. It had been years since Joah had operated a vehicle, but his movements were mechanical. He was *made* for this kind of constant forward movement. If only the miners could find more fuel for the tanks, more steel and latex for vehicle repairs...

Misla Crane, shattering his thoughts again, made a second stab at conversation.

"I know I look old for a graduate. I'm twenty-six. But I used to live with someone who didn't want me to be a retriever, so I had a late start."

She smiled at him. Joah kept his eyes on the High Road, fingers curled tight around the steering wheel. The sound of the bells had been swallowed by chirps, buzzing, and the swishing of grasses in the wind. It didn't help that Misla had rolled down her window, so that warm air channeled inside, thrashing their hair and stinging their eyes.

"Are you going to ask why I decided to become a retriever anyway?" Misla said after a stretch of silence. The sleeves of her uniform flapped in the wind and whipped her in the face.

"No," Joah said.

"And why not?"

"I already know how the story'll go." Joah had made up his mind that it would be best to quiet her. He had no interest in entertaining strangers with polite chattering, especially if that snaking whisper of a *word* was going to be tossed into the conversation as casually as sugar cubes in tea. "You realized your 'true worth' or 'full potential' or something fantastically uplifting like that. Frankly, I don't really care."

This, apparently, wasn't enough to quiet Misla Crane. As the High Road crested a hill and they rattled downward between patches of tall, swaying shrubs, she snorted with giggles.

"That was a good one, Detective Cadshaw. I get it. You want to play asshole."

Joah tightened his grip on the steering wheel. He didn't answer.

"Look," she said, "Your cranky mask doesn't frighten me, okay? I know you're unhappy about doing this mission, because last time you came back from retrieving, your wife—"

"Stop," Joah said.

"And I really *am* sorry about your wife." Misla's hair flapped backward as the wind gushed through her open window. "It was horrible, what happened to her. I was there when it happened, you know. In the crowd. I—"

"Stop it," Joah said. His old anger flashed beneath his ribcage.

"But I bet you missed getting away, seeing the parts of the world we pass so quickly through," Misla continued rapidly. "It's part of the reason I—"

Joah roared. He rammed a foot on the brakes, and Misla Crane was finally quiet.

They had turned around a bend. A sea of white, like a blinding cloud, blocked the High Road before them, cutting across their path just like that vicious red slash on Deckler's map. In the midst of the white, thousands of curled slices of orange glowered at them.

"Are those...?"

"Birds," Joah grunted.

It was a horde of them, perched on the High Road and in the grasses surrounding them: skeletal, leathery, and blinding, it was as if their skin had been slapped by the moon. Their beaks were sharp and pale, but their eyes were like curved slits of sunset-orange.

"Well, there's your Traffic Control, Crane," Joah muttered.

"I've... I've *seen* these birds before," Misla said, hushed. "Among the cotton trees at the edge of the forest. Right before we passed that tower General Deckler was talking about. They were picking at the cotton. For nests, I think."

As they stared, one of the birds gave a crowing warble. Joah squinted at it. He *hadn't* seen these creatures before, but he knew at once what they were doing in the grasslands: their homes, the cotton trees, had been drowned out by the thirty-year night.

The birds were Moving.

"Misla," Joah said quietly, "roll up your window."

"What?" She turned to look at him. He saw himself reflected in her pupils, and was momentarily distracted. But then his peripheral vision caught movement among the birds.

"Roll up your fucking wind—"

As if this were a signal, the birds on the High Road burst toward the vehicle like a white sea. More exploded from the shrubs, their leathery wings flapping like boat sails. Before Joah could so much as twitch, one had stuck its neck through

Misla's open window and begun tugging at her shirt with that pale, curved beak. Its wings thumped against the side of her door.

Joah punched his pedal to the steed's floor and ripped through them. There was a dull series of *thuds* as the ones before them were pummeled, but then Misla was screaming. The bird clinging to her hadn't let go; its wings flapped frantically as it tugged at her uniform, and now more birds were poking their necks through the window, screeching.

They wanted cotton.

"Your shirt. Just give them your shirt!" Joah said.

Misla shrieked as the bird ripped a strip of cloth from her body. One-handedly, Joah ripped off his own tunic and flung it into the abyss of snapping beaks, hoping it would satisfy them, but they only continued pecking at her, and now he was almost veering off the High Road.

He jerked the wheel back. Left and right, those curved beaks rammed into the glass, causing pebble-sized chips in the windows. A sudden violent *crack* in the windshield obscured Joah's vision, and he swerved to narrowly avoid a crooked tree bowing over the High Road. Misla panted, practically playing tug-of-war with her shirt now. One of the birds had ripped it until it resembled a frayed blanket, but she hugged a sleeve to her bare chest.

"Let *go*," Joah hissed. "Let go, dammit."

"No, no, no," she said, gritting her teeth.

Cursing, Joah reached across her lap and helped jerk her arm back inside. He twisted her window crank until the glass slid to a close. The birds were dispersing now, many having been bashed by the steed's steel mouth, others flapping out of harm's way, unable to keep up.

Misla sat back, panting. All that remained of her shirt was a tattered slip of fabric draped around her left shoulder. Her neck and arms had been pierced in various places, the bleeding cuts like oozing half-smiles, but Joah's gaze was inadvertently drawn to her chest: right beneath the underwire of her torn bra, a burn scar as big as a dinner plate marred her skin. It was a raw, flaring pink, bumpy and textured with lines like veins.

"Go ahead, keep staring," Misla muttered, crossing her arms over her breasts and looking out the window as the last of the birds gave a final squawk and fell behind. "You're the first one to see it. I hope you feel honored."

Joah forced himself to focus on the twisting road before him as they bounced over rocks, his cheeks warm with the guilt of looking at something she had so obviously tried to hide. He wanted to tell her to put some antiseptic on the fresh cuts, but his words got tangled on the way out of his mouth.

"What happened?" he asked quietly, fully expecting her not to answer.

She surprised him, wiping her tears with her remaining slice of sleeve.

"When I left my partner a few years ago, he—he didn't want me to leave."

"Didn't want you to..."

"Leave, yes. He threw a lantern at me. It shattered and... well, you can see what it did."

Lantern. The word was vaguely familiar. Joah imagined orange, sparkling glass.

Misla smiled weakly.

"It's what the miners invented to see underground, where the sunlight can't reach. He—my ex's dad had been one. A mineworker. My ex, he liked to remember his dad by nailing these thick black blankets over all his windows to keep the house dark. Like a cave. He lit candles and oil lamps for light. He taught me how to make fire out of friction and a whisper.

But then I decided to leave, and—well, he decided to use his light against me."

Joah felt his jaw pop. He was suddenly glad, for the first time since joining, that he worked for the law enforcement office instead of the retrieving unit now.

"What's his name?" he said immediately. "I can turn him in when we get back. Unless—did you already tell someone? Is he in jail? If not, Crane, I can put him there."

But Misla just smiled. As they bounced over a rut, she covered her chest with her hands, smearing blood on the top of her chest. "I think it's a little too late for that. But thank you."

Joah swallowed thickly. He had the rest of this mission to convince Misla to report her abuser. For now, she needed bandages to stop the bleeding.

"There's a red case in the back," he said, eyes flickering toward the cuts on her arms and hands. "You'll find some tape and antiseptic cream in there. And take a couple of those green capsules while you're at it. It'll relieve the pain."

"I don't need—" Misla began.

"*Now*, Crane," Joah growled. "Deckler told you to do everything I say. Find a couple of new shirts for both of us while you're at it too. I packed some in my duffel."

She relented and turned, rummaging in the back. As the ravine to their right sunk lower, however, and the hills to their left became steeper, a flash of green caught Joah's eye. It was brighter than the deadening grass around them, a color he recognized as the exact shade of green the community seamstresses had collected from hillside plants and made into dye in the last year.

He slowed. Parked the steed. There were no signs of the cotton birds. Still, he peered in all his mirrors, ignoring Misla's inquisitive, flushed face, before hopping out and crunching over to what lay like an alien lizard in the dirt, the air stale and brittle against his bare back.

It was part of a ripped shirt, ripped like Misla's had been. It showcased the left side of a cat's slender yellow face. The spray of loose yellow threads was like drooping whiskers.

A green shirt with a cat on it.

His chest hammering, Joah bent and rubbed the fabric between his fingers. He looked around, but there was no sign of the boy who had once worn it—no sign of the boy who must have wandered this far west, who must have been ambushed by the same cotton birds they had. The last remnants of grass patches surrounding them were still.

Joah stood, clutching the shirt. The ice moon was mounting Aro's sky, reflecting UV rays with such intensity that the back of his head pounded. They would have to stop and sleep for a dozen arcsecs until the moon fell again, but as he returned to the steed and told Misla to prepare the beds, Joah had never felt less tired.

Lupita had been right. The Nocturnals had, for the first time ever, infected a child.

Numb, he let Misla take the half-shirt from him to examine it. Despite her earlier chatter, she didn't ask him why he had stopped to pick up a strip of kidnapped cotton. She only turned the fabric over and over. Her fingernails traced the cat's canines etched with white thread.

The Nocturnals have infected a child. The Nocturnals have infected a damned child.

Which meant Joah wasn't leaving the case of Damien Fertheli behind at all. He and Misla Crane were following the boy toward what everyone called the Eternal Night.

And they would, Joah promised himself, find him.

Sunset

"Hey, Hicks, get up. Retrievers are here."

Hickory Glade groaned in his bundle of blankets, thumbing his pounding temples. His tent-mate had poked his head through the open flap to wake him, but the ice moon was still hovering above the northern skyline, sending a stripe of brilliant white through the canvas.

"Retrievers?" Hickory said, sitting up. "What the hell d'you mean, retrievers?"

Scowling, he checked the timepiece strapped to his wrist. Unlike the rest of the Sunsetters, who started Moving when the sun hung ten degrees above the horizon, the miners didn't have to pack up until five: at five degrees, the sun dangled low in the sky and nighttime prowled just around the corner.

But the hand of Hickory's watch still hovered over the spindly number seven. Not quite late enough to start chasing daylight like they had to do every two damn years. *Strange.* Retrievers usually only showed up when someone—some hunter or scavenger or miner—had gotten lost out in the woods and needed their asses saved from the Eternal Night.

"Yeah, retrievers," Sid said, pushing aside the flap so that smoke and murmurs filled the tent. "Apparently they've got something to tell us. General D's orders. C'mon."

Hickory groaned, stretched, and cracked his neck with a swift jerk of his head. Something felt off, as if warning bells were clanging in the back of his mind. Loud voices and crude jokes usually speared the morning air, but now he only heard gruff whispers and rumbles, quiet, anxious words masked by the roar of the distant river that ran along the edge of their campground.

"Alright, alright, I'm getting up. Wait for me, asshole."

He shook away his blankets and pushed through the dew-slick flap, following Sid to the wooded area outside their caverns. Here, a crowd of soot-faced miners elbowed each other and craned their necks to look at whoever stood in the center of the clearing.

Hickory wasted no time, shoving past his comrades until he had squeezed his way to the front of the pack. He jerked to a gut-wrenching stop when he saw who the two retrievers were.

No, it couldn't be.

Joah Cadshaw. *Joah Cadshaw* was poised in front of the conglomeration of tents and ashy, smoking firepit, his hands clasped neatly behind his back. Hickory rubbed his eyes, but when he opened them again, the horrible apparition was still there. Cadshaw was dressed in a tight, plain white shirt, very different from the crisp retriever uniform he'd used to wear. His hair was ruffled, his chin stubbled, his frame skinnier than the last time Hickory had seen him.

And he, Joah Fucking Cadshaw, was standing elbow to elbow with—

"*Misla,*" Hickory spat, cutting through the low grumble of conversation.

When he said her name, the branches around them seemed to still, and the beetles scuttling up their trunks seemed to slow. The distant river, however, thundered with the spite thudding through Hickory's veins. Angry, white foam filled his chest.

"What the hell are you doing here? With *him*?"

The miners coughed themselves into awkward silence. Joah Cadshaw spotted him with the faintest spike of surprise, eyebrows lifting a fraction and narrowing again.

Misla Crane couldn't stifle *her* shock, though. Tilting her head, she said, "Hickory?" in that sickeningly sweet voice she had always used around him, the innocent one. It made him want to throw her onto a bed and pound that silly innocence out of her.

"You two know each other?" Cadshaw asked coldly.

"Yes, you Nocturnal-loving freak, Misla and I *know* each other." Hickory lurched forward, but rough hands cupped his shoulders, holding him back. "She was my girl. She was *mine*, and now you've taken her, just like you took everything else from me. Let me *go*."

But Sid's hold only tightened, and Hickory's worst memory swirled before him:

It was thirteen degrees. He stood in the middle of the High Road before the executioner's block, his ax glinting in the sun. People lined the road in thick rivers of hot bodies and excited whispers, watching as the retriever in the distance led his prisoner toward them. An Infected's execution was usually an exciting ordeal, but this time it was even more so: it was the retriever's own wife *who had been infected, the retriever's own* wife *Hickory would kill.*

He licked his lips, tasting the salt of his own sweet sweat. He'd never liked Joah Cadshaw. Ignorant, cocky prick. If he could pull the man's guts through his neck and dangle them around his own, he'd wear the necklace every damn arcsec. It served him right, in a way, that the Nocturnals had chosen to infect Blair Cadshaw. They picked one victim a year to lure to their shit-pit of never-ending darkness; Retriever Cadshaw had always tracked these victims down with ease, forcing them back to their deaths before they could sneak back on their own and wreak havoc on the community. Hickory himself had never hid his fascination with his ax, but Cadshaw had always pretended to be repulsed by the whole ordeal. A reluctant hero.

Until now.

Now Hickory could see, as Cadshaw and his chained wife drew nearer: the famous retriever was actually *repulsed. Pain twisted his face. When he finally reached the executioner's block, he* addressed the man sitting behind Hickory's post, desperation in his voice.

"I beg you to reconsider, General. I think she's trying to tell us something."

At his words, the woman opened her mouth and screamed, "WARN. WARN. WARN." Drool swung from her teeth. She looked as insane as all the other Infected scum Hickory had gotten rid of before, but behind him, General Deckler made a grunt of pity.

"I can postpone the execution if you have sufficient proof that she is not dangerous."

"What?" Hickory spat, spinning around.

The general had always loved Joah Cadshaw, true, but why was he falling for such a biased pile of shit? Even as Hickory watched, the Infected woman swiped a pale, clammy hand toward the onlookers, that drool soaking through her shirt.

No, she was still dangerous. Cadshaw would put them all at risk because he would never quit loving the monster his wife had become.

"I'll consider a life extension," General Deckler began, but Hickory marched forward. Before Cadshaw could blink, before the crowd could gasp, he raised his weapon. The blade sliced cleanly through *the Infected woman's neck. Her head hit the ground with a thud.*

A shivering silence.

Then Cadshaw was screaming. He threw himself forward and tried to wrestle the ax from Hickory's hand. His eyes bulged, and Hickory clung to his ax like a lifeline, and they threw each other to the High Road, rolling in Blair's blood, the blade narrowly missing Hickory's left ear...

General Deckler's men had jumped in to break them apart. Afterward, Hickory had been fired for misconduct, but Cadshaw himself had simply been transferred to another department for his own "mental wellbeing," or some soft-hearted, bullshit excuse like that. Hickory had watched in a drunken stupor as Misla, once an angelic little creature he'd wooed and won with all the right words, had packed her things and left him. He'd become like a headless pheasant, staggering around, making a wage by pounding grahsm from cave interiors like his father had once done. A regression in familial stance for sure.

"You lost me my job!" he said now, jerking against the arms wrapped around him. It wasn't fair that he, Hickory, was still out *here*, while Cadshaw had obviously wormed his way back into a retrieving position. Always General D's favorite, that was for bloody sure.

"Well, you killed my wife, so consider us even."

Cadshaw wasn't trembling, but his face had turned a blotchy, veiny purple that made Hickory feel triumphant. Oh, the mask was there, but it was slipping.

"Well, it looks like you paid me back, didn't you?" Hickory panted. "Looks like you've gone and stolen *my* woman. Is that why you left then, pretty girl? So you could be with *him*?"

He bit his lip. Tasted blood. His last encounter with Misla had not been pleasant, he had to admit, but she didn't look the worse for wear. She was wearing the same fitted white shirt Cadshaw was, but hers hugged her curves, and she had added a frayed scarf that bore a resemblance to the Retrieving Institute colors. She was plumper than he'd last seen her. Her hips were wider, her breasts lower, her cheeks rounder. A good weight gain. It added a flush to her face, a look of strength in her thighs.

But her eyes weren't flickering downward like they'd used to. They squinted at him with no trace of that soft, liquidy warmth he had come to associate with melting candle wax. These new eyes looked hard and gray and unyielding.

Before Hickory could say anything else, Misla cupped her hands around her mouth to address the crowd, as if his outburst had been nothing more than the irritating chirp of crickets.

"The Moving bells rang early because the High Road was severed."

At that word, *severed*, Hickory saw Blair Cadshaw's head at his shoes. The wisps of her hair brushing his ankles. Her blood soaking into the asphalt of the High Road.

"We have to stray from the road our ancestors have been using for centuries," Misla continued. "You all need to pack up immediately." She paused, glanced at Hickory, and cleared her throat, throwing a braid over her shoulder. "It's been easy to follow the sun our whole lives, because we can travel four times as fast. But this detour will slow us down. The Nocturnals won't be far behind."

"Any questions?" Cadshaw asked, his eyes trained on Hickory.

"Well, how come the High Road was severed?" someone called.

"We don't know," Misla said. "Possibly a quake. Some kind of natural disaster. Either way, it's going to take longer than expected to reach the Green Sea. So get Moving."

With that, *Hickory's* woman—yes, she was still Hickory's woman, he felt that deep within him—whipped around with her new bravado and strode back through the path of trees, that frayed scarf bouncing on her neck, Joah Cadshaw on her heel.

The arms holding him back loosened. Hickory turned to see Sid raise an eyebrow at him as the rest of the miners burst into movement, tearing down tents and lugging supplies to the pack horses in another clearing through the trees.

"Sorry, Hicks, had to do it," Sid said. "Couldn't let you kill the nut. Though I guess if you had, there's no General Deckler around to fire you."

"Good Old General D's *obsessed* with Joah." Hickory licked the last beads of blood from the cracks in his lips. "I knew it back then—if Joah wanted to delay his wife's execution, Deckler wouldn't just grant the wish. He'd blow kisses into Joah's asshole too, for good measure." Hickory mimed a kiss without humor. "If I killed him now, the general would track me down and staple my face to his office wall, right next to that shiny Nocturnal poster of his."

Apparently, Sid decided this was funny, because he belly-chuckled. The tension cracked inside Hickory, who laughed with him, eyes tracking the last patches of Misla's new, widened ass as she pushed through branches and disappeared in the thickness of the trees.

"So," Sid continued when they had quit laughing. He spit into the nearest fire. A coal sizzled. "You ready to Move, Hicks? The city's so slow, we'll catch up to those slugs in no time. Might as well bring the shiniest grahsm with us. Get some extra silvers for it."

"Oh, I'm ready to Move," Hickory said, still gazing at the place where Misla had melted into the woods. He could practically feel her shrill breath in his ears again, but that may have been the sudden breeze whistling between the trees. "I'm not Moving toward the sun, though."

Sid's eyebrows reached his shiny, slick hairline. Hickory laughed.

"I can't let him steal her again. I'm going to get my girl back." He paused, imagining Aoif Deckler. "I think my face getting stapled to a wall is a risk I'm willing to take."

Joah and Misla left seven degrees behind them like an old, fallen-off shoe.

When they reached six degrees a dozen arcsecs later, the sun cast dark purple shadows; its rays had shrunk until it resembled a neat orange ball hovering inches from the horizon behind them.

"Oil scavengers should've started Moving by now," Joah told Misla, forcing himself to sound as if he hadn't just exchanged words with his wife's killer. "We'll probably pass them on the High Road. We've just got to make it to that tower near the oil reserves, make sure no one got left behind. Then we can head back."

"Right," Misla said.

Five degrees. They continued in dense silence. The stretch of forest and caves where the miners had been residing morphed back into tall, naked cliffs, as if they were entering a dead zone between two forests. Beyond the tower, Joah knew, the woods would rejuvenate.

Four degrees. They'd be passing the scavengers any moment, but Joah hardly cared. His whole being quivered with suppressed rage. Oh, why hadn't he just charged at the man? Why hadn't he finally killed the monster haunting his dreams? And why hadn't Misla mentioned it—that she'd dated such a beast? That *he* was the one who had burned and abused her?

I was there when it happened, you know, she had told him. *In the crowd...*

Three degrees. Dark shadows leapt across the High Road. *Hares*, Joah thought numbly.

Then the steed's magnetic clock read two degrees, the bright blue of the sky glistened with dark streaks of orange, and he couldn't restrain his words anymore.

"It was him—" he began.

He glanced at her. His breath caught on his tongue. Under different circumstances, the new lighting might have made her beautiful. But dried tears striped her cheeks, and those smile-shaped scratches marked the hollows of her neck, which she had tried to hide by wrapping the tattered remains of her retrieving uniform around her throat like a scarf.

"It was Hickory Glade?" he grunted, before he could swallow himself into more silence. "You dated him? He's the one who gave you your scar?" *And mine*, he didn't add.

Misla sighed.

"He was charming, at first. He always told me the most fantastic *stories*. Some were about his father. The miner. He told me all about his dad's adventures, how his dad had discovered magic metals and secret caves, how he would come home with beautiful stones for their rock collection. Hickory still had those stones.

He kept them in empty jars and placed them all around his house, and in the darkness lit by fire, it was all so...so *beautiful.*"

Joah knew for a fact that Hickory Glade had loathed his status as a simple miner's son, had only told these stories to glorify the poverty-stricken childhood he had grown up in.

"But most," Misla continued, and her next words came as no surprise, "were about his grandfather. The general before Deckler. He told me about his grandfather's rise to leadership. How he developed the warning system. How he died. Hickory talked a lot about how he died."

Joah knew that Hickory's grandfather had been killed by Nocturnals about six decades ago. But he couldn't force himself to conjure any pity. He stared ahead as the High Road made a sharp bend around a crag. With the light dimming, branches and twigs that jutted from the cliffs looked more and more like long, crooked fingers. There were occasional muffled hoots and far-off yowls that sounded like glitches in the normal noise of life.

"Listen, Joah," Misla said earnestly. "I left Hickory after he murdered your wife."

Murdered.

Chills wormed up Joah's spine at that word. Not killed. Not executed. *Murdered.*

He stared without seeing at the bluffs before them. Everyone else had considered his wife's death a violation of procedure. Hickory Glade had been fired for misconduct, not *murder.*

Yet, finally, here was someone who believed otherwise like him.

"I always suspected Hickory enjoyed his little executions," Misla continued in a deadpan voice. "He always convinced me otherwise. He told me it was for the good of the Sunsetters. He was saving children's lives. The Nocturnals and everyone they infected were demons that would infest our community if left untreated. It wasn't until he swung that ax before General Deckler's say-so that I knew he'd been lying. He *liked* killing. I could see it on his face when—well..."

"Yeah," Joah managed to choke out.

The crests of the distant mountains glowed purple, like the treetops had caught a violet fire. Migrating birds freckled the sky. At the thought of birds, Joah became distinctly aware of the cushioning in his back pocket: the remains of young Damien Fertheli's green cat shirt. Evidence that the Nocturnals had gotten into the head of a child.

Misla had asked about the shirt after they had scrambled into their sleeping bags three cycles ago, but he hadn't found the right words, had instead mumbled something about making sure she finish cleaning and wrapping her cuts. Now, though, after seeing the way she had addressed the miners so calmly in the face of her fanatic ex, he knew he had to tell her about the Infected boy.

He opened his mouth, but Misla spoke before he could.

"Anyway, I decided to become a retriever after I left Hickory. I've always hated how we behead the Infected as *soon* as we bring them back—"

"Not true," Joah retorted. The green shirt was pushed momentarily from his mind. "If we can drag them back before they reach... well, what you'd call the Eternal Night, we put them in a white room and wait to see if the madness subsides. Sometimes it does. More often it doesn't. But the public doesn't see that. The public only sees the Infected that managed to make physical contact with the Nocturnals, the ones who sneak back after a few years to ravage our community. Retrievers track down *those* ones before they can surprise-ambush us—"

"I know, Boss," Misla cut in. "I just graduated from the Retrieving Institute. I got top marks, you know. All that you just said was in our senior exam."

"Well, what's your *point*, Crane?"

"I want," said Misla, with a breath so deep it seemed to suck the air from Joah's own lungs, "to see if the Infected can talk to the Nocturnals and find out what they want."

Joah's heart thrashed against his ribs. All thoughts of telling Misla about the ripped green shirt in his pocket fluttered away, alongside the migrating birds overhead.

"Crane..." He tried to sound casual. "You don't think I tried talking to every single Infected person I brought back? You don't think I delayed missions to interrogate them?"

She looked at him. He kept his eyes pasted on the winding High Road. Fat rodents were pattering across their path now. He swerved to avoid running them over.

"You don't think I purposely ran out of fuel to give the Infected extra time to heal? You don't think I spent a whole *year* with my crazed wife out here in the wilderness trying to find a cure, only to fail, only for General Deckler to send more retrievers to force us back with a death penalty hanging over my head as well as hers?"

"I didn't—"

"Of course you didn't know." Snot clogged Joah's throat. "Everyone thinks retrievers are cold and cruel. But once the Nocturnals lodge their whispers into your head, they don't withdraw those whispers —but, of course, you'd already know that. Retrieving Institute, and all, right?"

"Look," Misla said, crossing her arms, "I know you're bitter. I know you're sad. But you don't need to treat me like—like—*scavengers*."

"Like scavengers?" Joah repeated.

"No. Look. Scavengers."

Misla pointed through their cracked windshield. During their conversation, the High Road had rounded a cliff and continued into a wide expanse of hardened, rocky aro. Now, perched on the opening beyond, the outline of a cylindrical tower bowed over the High Road.

But the High Road wasn't empty. Each strapped with bouncing silver canteens, sprinting toward them, were the oil scavengers who should have started Moving five degrees before. They were hollering indistinguishably, their voices like blunt knives failing to slice the air.

Cursing, Joah sped toward them until they were close enough to hear each gasping word.

"Hey, hey, hey!"

"Did General Deckler send you?"

"Thank God you're here."

Joah punched the brakes as they met the scavengers, who were coughing and panting. Their mops of hair were gray with dust. Their hands were slimy with oil and blood.

"Hold up." Joah tugged on the parking stick and jumped out onto the dusted High Road to meet them. "It's almost sunset. Why the *hell* are you lot still here? I thought you might've taken a shortcut and that's why we didn't see you on the High Road, but I never thought—"

"Mack got killed," one scavenger piped up, breathless. "He's my friend, Mack is. *Was*, I mean. A night beast came braver than usual. Tiptoed into sunset. It got Mack—"

"And all our damn horses," another scavenger added.

"Aye, and all our horses," the first scavenger agreed, "it's like nothing I've never seen in my life. Like a cat, but bigger, and it's got scales."

"The night beast is some kind of reptile, you mean?" Misla asked.

All the men's eyes flashed over to her, as if they had permission now that she had spoken. They scanned her body for much too long, some with smirks.

"I guess," said the scavenger, his eyes on Misla's chest, "but a cat-like reptile."

"And how did this creature kill your friend?"

"It yowled at 'im. Horrible yowl, could've burst your eardrums. And Mack dropped to the ground, screaming and twitching. And then the cat drug him away into the forest by its claws. Same with the horses."

Joah and Misla exchanged glances. A grim understanding shot between them.

"You're sure it was a night beast?" Joah asked.

"Aye. Stayed in the shadows the whole time. Not that that's too hard, with the forest a little way back, and the tower. That tower makes a *long* shadow."

The group all turned to gaze at the strange construction, which looked, Joah thought, like a giant canine tooth, fat and round at the bottom, tapered and sharp on top. It was far larger and more permanent than anything the Sunsetters had ever created in living history. It had been quite the object of horror stories and conspiracy theories as they had passed it during the last Move, but General Deckler had been firm about Moving by, not staying to investigate. Only after they had settled had he sent some men back to collect the oil in a nearby reservoir.

"Can we ride back with you?" the first scavenger asked now. His canteen was dripping beads of that oil onto the dirt of the High Road. "We could cram in the back if we threw some stuff out." He peered through the window. "You don't need them tents if we head back now, and we'd only need 'bout half those cans if we ration. Should make it back in three cycles, yeah?"

Joah and Misla passed that knowing look again. Dimly, Joah felt warm surprise that they could already communicate the vague basics without speaking.

"You won't make it back before three moon cycles," Misla said firmly. "And Retriever Cadshaw and I aren't going back just yet, so no, you can't hitch a ride with us."

"Come again?" the scavenger asked.

"The Sunsetters already Moved." Briefly, Joah explained the fissure in the High Road. "Retriever Crane and I are going to investigate the creature that killed your friend. If the night beasts are starting to chance sunlight, General Deckler needs to know about it."

And we need to search for the boy, he didn't add.

"We'll give you some of our food," Misla said. "If you stick together and keep a steady pace, you should be fine. Just veer right after the grasslands. You might even catch up to the grahsm miners, they just left and there are a lot more of them, so they'll be slower than—"

Joah saw it coming a second before it happened.

The first scavenger tilted his head, his eyes flickering toward his mates, his pupils gleaming with that dog-like hunger for survival. His lip curled upward. His mates gave wisps of laughter, like schoolgirls giggling behind polite hands when a boy is doomed for detention.

"Crane, DOWN," Joah bellowed.

Misla didn't hesitate. She thudded to her knees; the scavenger's swinging fist missed her head by an inch, but another one, shiny with oil and dirt, met Joah's ear.

His skull exploded. His lungs seemed to jump out of his throat. Boots connected with his body from every direction. The High Road pounded his spine again and again, like a crazed, violent mother burping her baby. Dust heated his throat.

Far off, Joah thought Misla might be climbing the shafts of orange light in the sky like a stairwell, screaming his name. *Strange.* He couldn't remember who Misla was, exactly, but he thought perhaps she was his wife. Perhaps she was beautiful.

Then the scavengers gave his ribs a final kick, and the Eternal Night folded him in its calm, cold embrace.

Sleep cocooned him. No light disturbed his darkness and no sound punctuated his silence. It was as if he lay in a black pond, where the waves lapped over him seamlessly, lulling him into a cavern where light and sound didn't exist. And there was no light and there was no sound. No light or sound. Light or sound. Light. Sound.

A dull pounding sensation hammered the back of his head. It was not light *or* sound, but a *feeling*, like a beam of bright noise thumping itself into his skull.

"Stop it," Joah muttered, swiping his hand at the beam.

"Joah," the beam said back.

His eyelids betrayed him, opening him up to a bright, noisy world. A woman was leaning over him, chanting his name over and over, the left side of her face blotched and purple. The ice moon beamed beyond her shoulders.

"Keep waking up, Joah," the woman said, and her name came to him.

"Misla." He tried to sit up. The world tilted. The waves came back and spiraled around him. The woman pressed a palm to his chest and forced him to lie back down.

"Hey, hey, not so fast, take it slow, you'll be alright, just take it slow."

She said this all very fast, and her urgency cut through Joah's haze in a way the moon's ferocity couldn't. He blinked. He gazed at the bruise masking her left eye and cursed.

"They hit you," he mumbled. "The scavengers. Scum. Vultures. They hit you."

"They did a lot worse to you," Misla said. "I only wish I could've broken all their bones before they ran off. But I— there were too many of them. I think I knocked out a tooth, but..."

Her eyes darted left and right. For the first time, Joah became aware of how bright the moon was, stamped against the blackening purple sky. He tilted his head to find the sun, but it had shrunk to half a dome peeking between two cliffs behind them—a bloodred eye peering at them cruelly. Preparing to blink into nothingness.

"They took the steed, didn't they?" Joah spat, using his elbows to prop himself up.

Every inch of him ached. He did a quick self-evaluation and guessed he was concussed, with bruised ribs and a broken nose. Dried blood caked his upper lip. His jaw throbbed.

"Yes, they took the steed. Didn't leave us any food, either. They told me to kiss the sun's fiery red ass goodbye."

"How thoughtful," Joah growled.

"I know, right? Now, first things first, we need to get out of the open. If there really *are* night beasts lurking around, I'd rather not meet them for the first time with a damaged partner."

She paused, those eyes darting again. The noise of sunset swelled, but Joah couldn't tell where the creatures were, exactly; it sounded as if all the chirps and coos and cries were simply eddying around his head, ringing in his ears. As if the rocks were shrieking.

"I say we get to that tower," he grunted, nodding toward them. "I don't know if you got a good look when we passed by during the last Move. *I* didn't see any doors, but looks like it's made of metal. It'll retain the sun's heat long enough for us to form some kind of plan."

He huffed as he tried to stand. "After the sun sets, it can get cold. Fast."

"Okay, tower it is. But don't crap yourself trying to get up so fast. Let me help."

Misla placed her hands in Joah's armpits and hoisted him up. He bit his lip to keep himself from crying out, then gasped anyway as his teeth pierced an already mangled lip.

"Don't worry, you can make as much noise as you'd like. I won't laugh."

"You're too kind."

Misla's lips twitched as they hobbled toward the outline of the tower before them, Joah's arm hooked around her neck, the moon glowing brighter above them. Sometimes he glanced sideways and mashed his teeth together at the sight of the bruise that had spread from her eyebrow to cheekbone. When—*if*—they caught up to the rest of the community, he'd have Deckler throw the scavengers in the smelliest portable prisons, *that* was for sure.

Greasy, slimy sons of Dirt Slum bitches, he thought. *Cowardly piles of shit...*

But as the tower rose, grating the gray mob of clouds that had accumulated in the sky, Joah's internal curses gave way to a dizziness. His fingertips tingled. Even as Aoif Deckler's best retriever, he had only ever ventured this far into the darkness once before...

He was standing in a meadow. Clouds fragmented the sky, casting a bloody light on the stretch of never-ending grasses and tufts of violet wildflowers. A figure was swaying in the distance, walking away from him, chanting something indiscernible as she staggered westward.

"Almost there," Misla muttered. "Come on, just a little further."

Joah stared at the figure, knowing it was her. Her, her, her. The one he'd been chasing for a year now, the one who, the night before she'd run away, had whispered against his neck that she wanted to try for a baby soon.

"Joah, I—I think there *is* a door. Or some kind of opening. Look."

He tried to look, but *she had wanted to be a mother. Now she would never be a mother. She was a Nocturnal puppet, and Joah was almost too scared to call out her name. But he* did *call out her name, and despite what they said about the Infected's inability to understand language after the Nocturnals had twined words around their brains, she turned.*

She turned.

She turned, and Joah saw the face of his wife wearing a mask of purest white. Bright purple veins crisscrossed her cheeks and forehead, like shattered eggshells.

No, it was not his wife's face, but the ice moon posing as his wife's face. He felt a newfound tickle, like a stroking finger, caress the back of his neck. A dim part of him realized that the moon was king. Maybe not king of the day, but king of the Eternal Night. And now it had plastered itself over his wife's eyes, and it was laughing at him.

Her manic smile spread her cheeks as she hobbled toward him, arms outstretched...

"Stay with me, Joah, don't fall asleep yet."

Hazily, Joah saw Misla push through a blanket of wool-like cobwebs and help him through a rounded hole in steel, into a cavern of deepest pitch-black. Their shoes crunched over brittle objects scattered on the floor. Misla was saying something else to him, but he couldn't hear. Tingles scuttled up his spine, as if *his wife were in his arms now. She was laughing up at him. Her eyes twitched in their sockets, like a rat was squirming beneath her eyelids, desperate to break free and nibble at Joah's skin.*

Blair, *he cried.* Blair, Blair, Blair.

But she just laughed and laughed and squeaked, "Warn you. Got to," and then kept laughing, her tongue shooting in and out, her mouth so widely stretched he could see her uvula and each rotten tooth, and he knew then, although he would try to find her a cure later, that she was gone. Her body was here, but the Nocturnals had snatched her soul right out of his cradling arms. She was gone.

"Gone," Joah croaked. "Gone. All gone."

"What are you talking about, Joah? I'm right here. Just lean back. One moment."

Misla's warmth disappeared. He was alone, his back pressed against a smooth, cold surface. His head throbbed. When he pressed his hands against the floor to steady himself, something sharp pierced his right palm. He sucked in a breath that made his chest ache.

"Come back, Misla," he murmured.

She didn't answer. He blinked, trying to rid himself of the memories infecting him so that he could assess his present situation.

He was slumped against the wall of what felt like a smooth cave. But the mouth, through which streamed a glum pool of bruised purple light, was perfectly square, and there had been no caves surrounding the High Road. He had told Misla to take him to the tower.

Somehow, then, she had lugged him *inside* the structure. As his eyes adjusted to the darkness, Joah saw that there was a hole in the floor, like a giant toilet bowl that might flush away anything wandering in its path. And surrounding the hole in a swirl...

Bones. Tiny skulls. Bird beaks. The skeletons of hares, rats, and other animals Joah knew no name for.

"Misla!" he called, louder, his eyes racing toward that inexplicable entrance.

She appeared at the door, illuminated by a ball of fire. He stared, dazed, as she hurried inside, bringing the fire with her. That flickering kind of light was usually only used for cooking, but Hickory Glade must have taught her how to make torches, because Misla had wrapped the remaining slice of her retriever's uniform around a dead branch.

"Glad to see you're awake," she said, closing the door behind her. The bruised purple light gave way to dancing flames as she skirted carefully around the hole leading underground.

"Yeah, glad to be awake," Joah mumbled.

They gazed around them, Misla's firelight illuminating their surroundings.

Near the closed door, a stone staircase wrapped around the edge of the tower until it disappeared through the floor above. But Joah could not stop staring at the staircase that began at the edge of the hole in the ground and spiraled downward, into whatever abyss had been created beneath the tower.

"We'll—we'll be safe in here, I think." Misla started toward him, picking her way carefully so as to avoid stepping on skulls. "The night beasts can't get to us if—"

"But Misla, how did these *bones* get in here?" It took every ounce of determination to speak coherently. "I doubt all the sunset critters decided to have a death party inside a man-made building." Joah paused, his head spinning. "I...I just don't like this, Misla. Where'd that door *come* from? We—I—nobody saw any openings when we passed by during the Move."

"Maybe we all missed it." Misla bent down beside him. One hand still gripping the torch, she dug into her pocket and brought out a familiar green capsule. "Here, take this. It's the pain medication you wanted me to use after those birds attacked me."

"You didn't take—?"

"Oh, don't give me that look. It ended up working out. You need relief more than I did."

Joah grumbled, but swallowed the pill dry, realizing as he did so how his throat burned with a parched aridness. The scavengers hadn't even left them a water canteen, for God's sake. He opened his mouth to ask if Misla knew of any new curse words he could use, but she rammed a finger to her lips, nodding toward the ceiling.

A strange screeching noise, like grinding metal gears, echoed above them. Then came a *thump*, and a *clang*, as if something were banging two kitchen pans against each other.

Slowly, Misla bent and picked up a sharp, curved bone, holding it in a tight fist like a dagger. Her torch's fire danced and waved eagerly, its flames reaching toward the ceiling. Toward whatever night beast they had trapped themselves in this God-forsaken tower with.

Maybe it was the same reptilian beast that had hoarded all these skeletons, Joah thought with a barely suppressed moan. The same beast that had killed the scavenger Mack.

"Misla, what are you doing?" he hissed suddenly.

She had turned to creep toward the staircase by the door, torch in one hand, bone in the other. When Joah made to stand, she whispered, "I'm going to check it out. You stay there. You won't be able to help in your condition, so find yourself a sharp one and stay awake."

"Misla, *no.*"

But she was already climbing those stairs, which were steeper than the portable ones leading up to Aoif Deckler's office. They had no side railings, and Misla kept her shoulder pressed against the tower wall as she stole upward, around and around, until she had ascended to the landing above. Her absence brought a horrible, mud-thick darkness.

"Shit. Shit. Shit." Joah pressed his shoulder blades against the wall to scoot himself up. His body ached, but the sharp, dizzying agony he had expected did not come. The capsules worked fast, then, or else his panic had overpowered the pain.

Please be a hare, or a possum, or any kind of small, harmless creature, Joah pleaded as he limped his way around the hole and toward the staircase, hands outstretched in the darkness. But even as he lugged his foot onto the first stone step, he heard a shrill, keening wail above him.

"I'm coming, Misla, I'm coming!"

Now he was bounding up the steps, ignoring his body's aching protests. The staircase rose until it met a rounded opening in the ceiling, and then Joah was panting in a perfectly circular room lit with Misla's torch like the one below. Except there were no skeletons infesting this one's floor. Instead, spirals of steel hung from the ceiling, and Misla was crouching before—not a night beast—but a boy.

"Damien," Joah whispered, awe-struck.

The boy was naked, but so muddy it looked as if he had developed a new, thick layer of armor. Even so, Joah recognized his face as the same one plastered on sketches in his office. He also recognized the Infected wildness that had crept into the boy's eyes, the look of shattered eggshells and popping purple veins and a moon-like glow shrouding his features.

"You know him?" Misla demanded.

She had dropped her weapon, which lay discarded at the boy's feet. Damien was shuffling and panting. He seemed unsure of where he was. There was no hint of that wry smile that Blair had given, only a delirious confusion, the cries of a small babe calling for his mother.

"I—he's—his name's Damien Fertheli. He's—" Dazed, Joah reached into his pocket and brought out the limp scrap of green shirt he had plucked from the High Road. He held it out to the boy, then shook his head. "What the hell am I doing? Here, Damien."

He pulled off his own shirt. Tentatively, trying to keep steady, he slipped it over the boy's head. Damien only jerked away half-heartedly. A good sign. Joah grabbed the boy's hands—which were cold as the dead of night—and forced them through the sleeves.

The bottom hem unraveled to Damien's knees, so that, in the firelight, it looked as if the Infected child had donned a translucent, moon-woven dress.

Misla inhaled, but she wasn't staring at the boy. She switched the torch to her other hand and squinted at Joah's midriff. Damien let out another wail.

Joah looked down. His body glowed blue and green with bruises. They covered his ribs and chest like ripples in a pool. And suddenly it seemed as if the three of them, standing together, formed an eerie, indoor sunset: Misla, with her dwindling blaze of orange like the dying sun; Damien, in his egg-white dress like the ice moon; and Joah, the bruises painted over his body like the looming darkness that came with the Eternal Night.

Then Misla retracted her firelight. The spell was broken.

"How," she asked in a wavering voice, "do you know this boy? *How is he here?*"

Joah's legs couldn't hold him anymore; the pain had crept back into his head and lungs and ribs. He lowered himself to the floor as Damien wailed again.

"Do you remember when we first met? How Deckler told me to 'forget the boy'?"

Misla nodded, frowning.

"Well, this is the boy. This is the boy I was assigned to find."

In whispers, Joah told her everything, including Lupita Fertheli's suspicions that the Nocturnals had infected her son. Misla's frown deepened. When he had finished speaking, Damien began turning in circles, his wails morphing into decipherable mumbles:

"*West. West. Not scary. Scary. Going back. West. Need me.*"

"Honey," Misla said, taking Damien's hand. The boy flinched. "You can't go west. We're supposed to be going *east*, remember? We follow the sun. That's what we do."

"*Sun,*" Damien said. "*No. Scary. Going back. West. Need me.*"

Misla continued consoling him, but Joah stared. He had never witnessed an Infected person respond to conversation by repeating a word. *Sun,* Damien had told Misla, even though that had not been part of his original, mumbling vocabulary. Come to think of it, Damien was using a wider range of words than the Infected typically portrayed.

"Listen, Misla," Joah said urgently, "Damien's got a chance at returning to his old self. A better chance than most. But we need to figure out a way to get him home, and that's going to be pretty damn difficult without any kind of steed. We need to think of ways to—"

"The river," Misla cut in. She had coaxed Damien into a sitting position on the floor, where he rocked, mumbling his words, his hand still grasped tight by Misla's. "I've been thinking about it ever since the scavengers took off. It's the only way."

"That river by the grahsm miners?" Joah asked. "But we don't have time to build boats."

"What, are you afraid of getting a little wet?" Misla smirked. "We'll find some dead logs and float, of course. The river wasn't running parallel to the High Road, it was running—"

"Southeast," Joah said, excitement mounting within him. "The Sunsetters will still be heading south, so we'd run right into them! Yes. You're brilliant, Misla. If we start now, we might be able to reach the river before the sun's gone too far down." He hoisted himself up.

"Hold up. *You* need rest." Misla glared at him. "It's still moontime. We haven't slept in ages. And *he* needs washed." She nodded at Damien, who moaned.

Joah blinked at her. "How the hell do you expect to *wash* him without the river?"

Misla nodded at the twisted tubes of steel hanging from the ceiling like oddly misplaced rain gutters. "When I first came up here, I found Damien drinking. From those. Whoever built this place must have designed something on the tower roof to store rainwater for drinking purposes, because I think the water's clean."

"Well *that* would've been nice to know."

Joah hobbled to the nearest gutter, where a square metal container, almost like a mailbox, stuck out from the base of the tube. He lifted the hatch, threw his hands inside, and lapped the frigid water from his cupped palms.

Soon Misla couldn't seem to resist. She gently disengaged herself from Damien, who continued rocking on the floor, his arms hugging his mud-caked knees to his chest. Seconds later, Joah heard her gulping water from a neighboring gutter. He wiped his mouth on his wrist.

"Okay," he whispered. "How about this? We sleep for a few arcsecs. As soon as we wake up, we fill ourselves with water and head out. We'll have to keep a brisk pace, which might be..." He glanced at Damien uncertainly. Usually, the Infected struggled and fought against eastward travel. Sometimes they had to be lugged back in handcuffs or ropes. Damien, however, seemed momentarily uninterested in continuing his westward journey toward the Eternal Night.

Maybe because the darkness is already upon us. Maybe the Nocturnals are already here.

Shaking away this thought, Joah continued in a whisper, "He isn't showing any signs of trying to escape right now, but we'll need to watch him closely. And it might be hard to get him to cooperate in riding the river east."

"We'll manage," Misla said promptly. "C'mon, help me wash him."

Together, they brought Damien handfuls of water one cupped palm at a time, lathering it over his skin. The mud trickled away, revealing scratches and sores underneath. Joah tried not to cringe. The boy would need to be seen by a healer as soon as they reached the community.

When they had washed him as best they could, Joah caught Misla's eye and gave her a slow nod. She blew out her leftover fire, encasing them in a stony blackness. Joah heard the *clunk* of the torch as she set it down, and then they moved toward one another, feeling for Damien and each other's groping fingers. When they had found him, they settled onto the floor and eased the boy into a lying position, Joah pressing against his back and Misla hugging him from the front.

They grasped each other's hands so that the boy was swaddled in a tight cocoon. Now if he had the Infected urge to escape while they were sleeping, they would know.

"Who do you think built this place?" Misla whispered. She was so close, her breath puffed onto Joah's lips. Damien mumbled incoherently between them.

"I—I don't know. Whoever they were, they must have Stayed. You can't build something *this* big between Moves." Joah stared upward unseeingly, trying to imagine living thirty years in the constant light and thirty years in the Eternal Night. Who could endure *both*?

"Could've been the Sunrisers," Misla breathed. "These walls would protect them from night beasts, and the roof would protect them from the midday sun."

"Or it could've been the Leather Skins," Joah said, grunting as he moved his legs and renewed pain exploded in his ribs. The green capsule had worn off, then. "I'm sure there's enough insulation here to shield them from the cold of sunset and night."

"Or," whispered Misla, "it could've been the Nocturnals. We like to call them monsters, you know, but monsters don't have to be primitive. They could be really, really clever."

Of course, the Nocturnals who had been infecting Joah's people *couldn't* have built this particular tower: they'd been chasing the Sunsetters around the aro for the last six decades. But there were rumors of multiple communities of Leather Skins migrating at midday, so why couldn't there be a different community of Nocturnals who had built the tower instead?

Joah remembered the glossy poster in Deckler's office that he had tried not to look at: *that* hand-drawn imagining of a Nocturnal had been hunched, with many yellow eyes and pincers for hands and hunched shoulders, an insect-like beast incapable of creation.

But what if the insectile body straightened? What if the pincers shrunk into fingers and the eyes became two and the Nocturnal on the poster simply looked like his wife had, human, with a little cracked moon plastered over the skin of its face?

Damien was snoring between them now. Joah felt himself drifting. It had been a long time since he'd laid this close to other humans, since he'd felt this kind of warmth. Misla's hand was soft and small in his. In the darkness, it could have been Blair lying next to him, the child they had never conceived sandwiched between their bodies, safe and happy and alive.

"Dream well, Misla," Joah murmured before he let himself fall into this fantastic sleep.

"Damien? Where is he? *Where is he?*"

Misla's panicked voice snapped Joah from his grogginess. Fingernails pierced his bare chest, as if checking to see whether he was man or child. When Misla shifted away from him, crawling along the floor and screaming Damien's name, Joah sat up. His skull felt fit to burst.

"He's gone," Misla cried. "I don't know—how did we—? He was here! Right *here*."

"Okay. It's okay. We'll find him. He —"

But Misla was already moving toward the staircase. Her knees clunked against the floor as she crawled in the darkness. Joah blinked rapidly, as if his brain were trying to process the impenetrable indifference between opened and closed eyes. *This.* This was like rotten death.

"Hold up," he muttered, crawling after her.

He tried to clear his spinning head. They had fallen asleep trapping Damien between them. The boy must have disengaged himself and tiptoed away without waking them. But Misla had closed that enigmatic door downstairs, and the Infected were hard-pressed to figure out things like knob-turning or door-opening. Surely, Damien was still inside the tower, wandering like a drunken Dirt Slummer on one of the levels above...

When his hands found the topmost step, however, the darkness seemed to thin. Joah blinked and squinted downward, through the gap in the floor where the staircase curled to the ground. A scabbed strip of light—perhaps not even light, but a lesser darkness—spilled from an opening near the base of the stairs.

"Oh my God," Misla said beside him. She clapped her hand to the wall and stood on shaking legs. Together they crept downstairs: Damien *had* managed to open the door, which stood ajar like a missing tooth. Outside, the world had morphed into graying shadow.

"He's gone," Joah said, dazed.

He had been imagining Lupita Fertheli's tear-shined face when she saw her son again. The furious look Aoif Deckler would give when they told him the Nocturnals were infecting children. The revival of the boy when the healers tended to him and he returned to his senses under the sun. Now he and Misla Crane would return to the community childless.

"We need to go," he muttered. He felt numb, like his fingertips had melted away. "I think it's past sunset. Negative degrees." He checked his watch blearily. It was stuck at zero.

"Yes, I agree. C'mon, can you walk?" Misla grabbed Joah's elbow and began marching him across the floor. He staggered after her, their shoes crunching over fragments of bones. "I'm sure Damien hasn't gone far. If we hurry, we might catch him before—"

"Hold up. Wait. We're not going after him. Damien's gone."

Misla stopped and stared at Joah. Her hand fell from his elbow.

"We're not going after him?" she repeated slowly.

"No." Defeat sunk to the pit of Joah's stomach. "It's too late. We need to get to the river. Damien—there's a chance he'll find his way back in a year or so. The Infected usually do."

"The Infected *adults* usually do," Misla said, and her eyes seemed to flash with the reflection of last night's fire. "Damien is a *child*. Plus, in a year's time, if all goes to plan, we'll be sailing the Green Sea. He will *die*."

"No. *We* will die, Misla." Joah watched the way her jaw jutted out and knew that their survival would depend on her cooperation. He clenched his fists, steeling himself to hold his ground. "Listen to me, Crane. General Deckler told you to obey my every order."

"General Deckler isn't here, *Detective*," Misla hissed, and the word was a stinging reminder that Joah was no longer a retriever. "If you don't want to go after him, fine by me. But *I* wouldn't be able to live knowing I let a little boy walk into the clutches of—"

"And you're going to fight off the night beasts?" Joah said, his voice rising. "Or are you going to have a civilized conversation with the Nocturnals? Tell them to leave our children the fuck alone? Say please and thank you when they just hand Damien back to you?"

"It's none of your business how I'm going to do it." Misla's raised voice echoed throughout the rounded tower. She bent and scooped up what looked like a discarded jawbone on the ground, clutching it tight in a determined fist.

"Misla, no." Joah grabbed her wrist, but she wrenched away.

"Don't touch me, Detective Cadshaw."

And with that, Misla Crane paraded outside with her jawbone, into the graying twilight. Joah withdrew Damien's remaining strip of shirt from his pocket and hobbled after her, goosebumps erupting on his arms as the brittleness of the night air found his skin. If he had to tie Misla's wrists together and haul her back like he'd hauled so many of the Infected, he would, dammit. He'd do it for her own safety—

But the outside world hit him like an executioner's blunt ax. Even Misla, already halfway to the High Road, stopped in her tracks.

The ice moon glared with yellowed ferocity from the darkened sky, no longer a simple time-stamp for their sleep cycles, but a bowl of concentrated light partially hidden behind the clouds. Joah and Misla must have slept for more than a few arcsecs, then. They must have slept for an entire *cycle*, too stuck in the pits of their dreams to notice Damien's escape...

And the sun. The sun was gone. In the east, a faint ribbon of purple clouded the cliffs, but the light no longer extended to Misla or Joah or the tower. The High Road had been reduced to a black strip. Its surrounding shrubs, ablaze with chirping and buzzing, were mere shadows under the cloud-shielded moon.

"Misla!" Joah cried.

She had resumed her march westward, chin raised, free fist swinging at her side. She didn't turn at her name. When the old anger flashed beneath Joah's bruised ribs, he took out the fragment of green shirt from his pocket and let it fall from his fingertips, onto the dirt.

Fine. *Fine.* If she wanted to leave him, if she was so determined to enter the darkness like Blair had, then all the wrist-tying in the world wouldn't stop her. She was not Infected. She was free to choose. She was free to ignore his warnings, his experience, his knowledge of the night.

Joah turned on his heel, cursing at the ache in his sides. He wanted to scream, rip out his hair, beg Misla to come back, but her newfound absence was already weaving a different kind of pain throughout his chest.

Trying not to think of her or Damien, he scowled at the potholes riddling the High Road.

Damn road developers, he thought. *Lazy, arrogant bastards. Well, it's their fault trailer wheels and horse hoofs got stuck in these holes during the last Move...*

Joah stopped.

No, it couldn't be. He had imagined the sound. He'd been thinking about hooves, but the scavengers had claimed all their horses were dead; there couldn't be one here.

Yet the sound of clip-clopping grew louder. And between cliffs in the distance, two blemishes appeared on the horizon, trotting westward at an easy pace. Male voices resonated across the valley, so brash that the chirping around Joah faltered as it hadn't for him.

For a moment, Joah wanted to wave his arms in the air, holler for his and Misla's saviors. Maybe the presence of other people would revive her sense. Maybe Joah could still save her.

But then he turned to squint for Misla, who was only a far-off, swaying smudge, and he remembered the scavengers swinging a fist at her. He felt their boots against his ribs and tasted the copper of blood filling his mouth. No, he should be cautious this time around.

Before the men on horseback could spot him, he dove behind a nearby shrub, swiping away a lazy horde of bugs hovering around it. He lowered himself to his exposed belly and watched between prickly branches as the men drew nearer.

There were two of them, and their booming laughter renewed the goosebumps on Joah's arms. They didn't sound frightened in the presence of the infamous Eternal Night. They sounded *casual*, as if this were merely a school picnic. As if the moon were a silly plate of cheese they might pluck from the clouds. And one of their voices rang horribly familiar in Joah's ears:

"Gotta tell you, Sid, I never cared much for the heat anyway. Wish Deckler would let us hang out in the sunset zone. So much easier on the eyes, you know."

"Sure, and then we'd be living up to our *name*," snorted the other. "Why call ourselves the Sunsetters when we're so afraid of the sun actually setting?"

"Well," said Hickory Glade, "as soon as we find Misla and kill that bastard of a bitch she's been fucking around with, we'll go back and persuade everyone that nighttime is better."

Joah didn't dare exhale. He wished the insects would come back and swarm him again as Glade and the other miner passed his hiding place, their mares nickering when they were kicked onward. Dust ballooned in their wake.

Joah pressed a palm against his mouth to stop himself from coughing on the dust. The men were still close enough that he could hear their commentary on the tower, but his ears rang with Glade's previous words: *As soon as we find Misla and kill that bastard of a bitch she's been fucking around with...* Glade was going after Misla just as he'd gone after Blair. And maybe Misla could survive the Eternal Night for a few cycles until she realized her search for the boy was futile, but she wouldn't survive an angry man with an ax if he decided to use it.

An icy resignation sagged Joah's shoulders: he wouldn't be returning to the light of day.

He would *not* let Blair's murderer take another woman he had grown to care for.

The cough escaped him, but Glade was too far past to hear him now. He and his comrade were already smudges like Misla had been, and Misla herself had dissolved into the distance. Clouds now shrouded the moon completely, and Joah could barely make out the edge of the forest he knew lay on the lip of the west.

Hurry, Misla, hurry, he urged, scrambling upward. *Lose yourself in the cotton trees before they can find you.* And then, before he could reject the thought— *I'm coming for you.*

He cast a last look at the purple remnants of sunrays in the east, then turned his back to it and started down the High Road: toward Misla, toward Damien, toward Hickory Glade and the Nocturnals and whatever else lurked out of sight. The air frosted his bare skin.

Far off, in the forest, a night beast yowled.

Dusk

Wisps of cotton still hung from the trees like ghost tears.

It was these, more than the ice moon wrapped in clouds, that lit Misla's way into the forest, which seemed to swallow the High Road like a dark, greedy mouth might swallow a foreign tongue. The cotton glowed, almost as if the trees had absorbed and hoarded the last sunrays before the Eternal Night covered the world in its inky black cloak.

"Damien," Misla whispered.

When only rustling and chirping and hooting answered her, she veered off the High Road, into the cotton trees where she wouldn't feel as exposed. Or as *watched.*

Just keep the High Road in sight, she told herself. *It's your path home.*

She kept her fingers on the bark of trunks as she passed through them, her left hand clutched firmly around a jagged, curved bone. Her heart thumped in her mouth. She had to find the boy. Just *had* to. For three long years, she had trained to rescue the people the Nocturnals hypnotized and lured into the Eternal Night. She had known she might fail— General Deckler had warned his pupils of this grim possibility—but she had not expected to fail a *child.*

"Damien... Damien, are you there?"

The branches around her thickened as the cotton trees gave way to pines. Needles scratched her skin and the blossoming underbrush clawed at her ankles. She plunged onward, whispering the boy's name, not daring to shout in case her cry attracted a night beast.

And then something swooped overhead, sending prickles down her neck. Wings flapped against branches. The yellow pinpricks of eyes glowered at her from a tangled mass of trees, and there came a high-pitched, rasping yowl from somewhere to her left.

"Misla! Misla, where are you? Misla!"

The voice came from behind her. Misla, momentarily frozen in panic, uprooted herself and stumbled away from the howling, toward the High Road and Joah's calls.

She had not wanted to think of Joah Cadshaw, to even mention his name inside her head after he'd refused to retrieve the boy with her. But now her mind was racing with images of her partner's bruised and broken face. Her heart crashed against her chest.

He came for me. He didn't leave me. He's here. He came back for Damien. He—

The snorts of horses jolted her in her tracks. Horses? The scavengers had said their horses were *dead*, but there was no denying that steady *clop clop clop* of hoof against cobble. Misla stared through the cracks in the trees as what seemed like the carcasses of two mares rose from the rubble of the High Road. They burst through the branches, stampeding toward her with flaring nostrils and gleaming white eyes and flattened ears.

"Joah!" Misla cried. The bone slipped with sweat in her hand.

"I'm here, pretty girl."

There was a blaze of fire, and he appeared, his face shining with glee behind a cylinder of flickering glass. But it wasn't Joah. It was *him*, her ex-lover, the one she'd tried so hard to escape: Hickory Glade, straddling a mare, holding a lantern that looked horribly like the same one he had once swung toward her stomach, shattering its glass against her ribcage and watching with beady, unforgiving eyes as the flames devoured her shirt, as the oil melted her skin, as she screamed herself into oblivion. Now, in the lantern's twitching shadow of light, Hickory's warped features looked exactly like the night beast Misla had been imagining.

"Hickory," she choked out. "What—what are you *doing* here?"

She glanced behind him, at a second horse and the man astride it. He looked vaguely familiar. Misla guessed he had been in the clearing when she and Joah had delivered the news about the early bells. The miner's forehead shined with lines of grease. He licked his lips at the sight of her, as if in lieu of waving.

"I should ask you the same thing," Hickory laughed. "I didn't know Good Old General D sent you to the buttcrack of night. I mean, *look* at you, Misla, stumbling 'round in this darkness. That's one good thing about mining, huh, Sid?" He beamed at his companion. The lantern swung in his hand. "We know our tunnels and caves. We know how to live in the dark."

Misla swallowed thickly, fingers tight around the slick surface of the bone. Yes, Hickory had known how to live in the dark even *before* he had become a miner. She remembered the first time he had brought her over: his house had been dim and sweet-smelling, like moss rotting in a cavern. He had made her dinner in the candlelight, and, after a few drinks, told her of his dad's explorations in the various caves across the aro and his grandfather's adventures as the leader of their community before his untimely death. He'd even let a few tears slip down the hook of his nose. It had all lulled Misla into Hickory's personal cavity of darkness.

And now he was here, in front of her, trying to reel her in again five years later.

"I told you to Move, Hickory," she said, her throat dry, as if she'd swallowed the cotton she'd left behind. "General *Deckler* told you to Move. You disobeyed."

She tried glaring him down, but the hypocrisy of her own words made her lips tremble. Chuckling, Hickory slid off his horse with an easy grace. He tossed the lantern to Sid, who caught it by its rusted handle. Then he groped in his saddle pack and withdrew a glinting ax.

"Hickory, what are you—?"

"Where is he, Misla? Where's your shiny new retriever buddy? Thought I'd say hi, see."

Hickory stepped toward her, part of his face leaping with the light of flame, the other melting into the darkness. Misla's back hit the thorny fingers of a pine. She could smell the cloud of alcohol wafting from his open mouth: a bad sign at sunset, an even worse sign at night.

"H-he's taking a piss. Joah is," she said. "He'll be back soon, though, and then..."

She squinted over her shoulder as if she could spot Joah through the trees. Her heartbeat rose in her throat like vomit. The smell of Hickory's breath engulfed her. Before she could flinch away, he was inches from her face, grinning down at her with that ax in his fist.

The ax that had killed Joah's wife.

Misla didn't hesitate. She swung her bone toward the soft hollow of his neck. Hickory jerked away. The bone slashed his shoulder instead, and blood peppered Misla's lips.

"You *bitch.*"

Hickory flung his ax to the ground and grabbed Misla's hands with bone-crushing force. She dropped her weapon with a yelp. Pain exploded up her wrist. She heard *cracks* as her fingers snapped inside his fists, but Hickory laughed. Sweat oozed from the stubble on his upper lip.

"Why don't we speed up his return a little, huh?"

Hickory wanted, she realized with a sickening pinch in her stomach, to hear her scream for Joah as he tore her clothes from her body. His upper lip always gleamed with sweat when he wanted to get violent, when he wanted Misla to make noise. But Joah was nowhere nearby, and Misla would not give him the satisfaction of screaming—not anymore.

He flung her to the tangled forest floor. She caught a lopsided view of his companion; the man was still holding his glass container of fire, watching them with a greasy smirk.

"You're just going to *let* him, are you?" Misla cried at him. Hickory had found the buttons on her pants and was popping them off their threads.

"Ah, Sid likes stuff like this, don't you, Sid?" Hickory panted. "In fact, Sid, you can have this treasonous little bitch before I do. C'mon, then, it's not like she's new and clean anymore. I pounded that innocence out of her a long time ago."

This is what real darkness is, Misla thought as Sid blinked stupidly; his lips spread in a smile. He clambered off his mare to swagger toward them with his wobbling fire. Hickory's fingers were nailing her wrists to the ground. He had pinned her lower body with the crushing force of his thighs. *Fight them, hurt them, kill them,* Misla begged herself.

But when Sid approached, the two men swapped fire for Misla with ease. A dank, buzzing numbness had sprouted from her broken fingertips to her brain. She could not remember how to thrash or scream or do anything but lie there, letting them.

Sid was ripping her pants. He was touching her. Hickory was laughing in his drunken gurgle. The ax glinted a few steps away. The discarded bone glowed white just beyond it. Above them, the dotted orbs of birdlike eyes watched the proceedings with yellow apathy...

And Joah's voice was screaming her name in a distant world. Damien's muddied face swam above her. There were shouts. A *ping.* The pressure inside her released, but the full weight of Sid's body slumped against hers with a muffled *thump* that knocked the air from her lungs.

Misla gulped for breath. A slender steel dart stuck from the side of Sid's skull. His eyes stared vacantly at her chest. Hot blood pebbled her forehead.

Men were shouting, but their mingled voices ceased to matter when Misla craned her neck and saw *him* standing over her:

Damien. The boy she'd come to find.

And he wasn't alone. Surrounding him, dressed in what could only be snowflakes or stars, willowy figures held what looked like wands, their dark silhouettes somehow sharp against the nighttime forest, their eyes stamps of furious, glowing violet in the night.

Damien, Misla knew even as that darkness pummeled her to sleep, had found them.

He'd found the Nocturnals.

☼

The mares screeched and fled when Joah burst between their flanks.

His old anger returned with the swiftness of a hot knife when he saw the two men. They were bearing down upon Misla's limp figure buried halfway in scrub.

Without thinking, he lunged forward and scooped up the ax glinting in the brush. He held it high over his head and stumbled toward Hickory, who was mid-turn, the ghost of a laugh still wrinkling his face in the lantern's leaping light.

For a trembling moment, their eyes met. Joah imagined doing what he should have done three years ago. Swinging that blade down on his wife's killer. Ending his rotten life.

But the man thrusting himself into Misla had not turned, had not seen, had not stopped, and Misla was deathly silent, and Joah turned to bring the blade through *his* neck instead.

Goosebumps. A *ping*.

The man slumped onto Misla, dead, before he could bring the ax down.

A tornado of crisscrossing light whirled around them. Joah whipped around, disorientated by the sudden flare in glowing lines. He felt the ax wrenched from his grip. Hickory roared. A cold pinch of metal snaked around Joah's wrists. Icy sharp fingers—like talons—closed around his arms, locking him into place.

"No. *No*. Misla!" he screamed.

Something—a piece of the swirling puzzle of light—had broken apart from the others and was now hauling Misla upward by her armpits. When she stirred, the whirlwind of activity slowed around them, and Joah could see that figures circled them, illuminated by their own glow.

Everything, even Misla, was smeared from his mind when the eddying stopped and his eyes became accustomed to this terrifying new light.

Each figure's skin was a rich, blackish-blue that seemed made of the fabric of dusk, but glowing spirals, swoops, and lines etched their bodies like luminous tattoos. The effect was blinding, dizzying. It made them blend together, so that Joah had to squint to make out their individual faces. They had beaked noses, elongated arms that looked vaguely like wings, and tiny purplish feathers sprouting from where eyebrows would be.

No, it couldn't be.

They looked nothing like the buggy humanoids imprinted on General Deckler's poster in his office. Joah felt faint with unease; for a moment, he tried to tell himself that these people poised before him could *not* be the Nocturnals who had infected his wife and so many others in his community, not with the intelligence shining beneath the feathered frames of their faces.

Then one of them stepped forward—*male*, Joah somehow knew. Like the rest of them, he only had two eyes, and each one was a striking violet. He was clutching Hickory's lantern with those curved, talon-like fingers, while his free hand rested on the bony little shoulder of—

"Damien," Joah choked, twitching forward. The icy grip on his arms tightened. The truth lodged itself in Joah's throat like he'd tried to swallow a broken wristwatch. No other night beast besides a Nocturnal could have lured the Infected boy to their circle.

Damien was still wearing Joah's t-shirt like a skull-white dress. He wasn't shaking or rocking anymore. He gazed calmly and curiously into Joah's face. Then he looked at Misla, who was straightening in her captor's grip, and Hickory, who was still thrashing and cursing against the Nocturnal who held him.

Finally, Damien Fertheli glanced at the dead man lying curled at their feet, the slender dart jutting from the man's head like a single antler. He pointed at the corpse.

"*He*'s the only one who never worked for General Deckler."

If Damien hadn't opened his mouth, Joah would never have believed that these coherent words had flowed from his lips. Even Hickory fell silent to gape at the Infected boy, who had paused, gazing upward at the Nocturnal still gripping his shoulder.

"Yes, I know," Damien said eventually. He turned back to Misla and added, as if in explanation, "They don't tolerate what that man did to you here. Someone will take care of you when we get back to the others. But Prince Kal still wants me to—yes, okay."

Joah's mind reeled, trying to absorb the new information. All the other light-tattooed figures seemed to be looking at the lantern-holding Nocturnal as if he were their leader. Prince Kal. *Prince.* An insane chortle almost escaped his tongue. Oh, how General Deckler would have pissed himself laughing if he'd known the Nocturnals practiced a monarchy.

His strange mania died when Damien stalked toward Misla and peered down at her.

"This one here works for Aoif Deckler now," the boy told the prince Nocturnal, who cocked his head like a hawk examining a mouse. "She wanted to drag me back when she found me in the fuel tower back at sunset. She wanted to stop me from reaching you."

Misla whimpered. Damien moved toward Joah.

"This one *used* to work for him. He was the one who kidnapped so many of the bilinguals. He'd force them back to the community. To their deaths. My friends and I used to watch him lead the bilinguals back in handcuffs before our last Move."

Joah's throat had never been so painstakingly dry. Before he could attempt to speak, Damien moved to Hickory, who scowled at him. The boy's voice took on a frosty, forbidding quality that kissed Joah's neck with fresh goosebumps.

"*This* one beheaded the bilinguals. My mom didn't know, but I would sneak into the crowd and watch each time he did it. He would've killed me if he still worked for Deckler and I'd been forced back. He'd kill me right now, if he could. He brought his ax."

A flock of creatures swooped over their heads before Hickory could respond. Branches jostled around them. The pinholes of eyes blinked at them between trees, little half-moons that reminded Joah, inexplicably, of Lupita Fertheli.

"Damien," he said, ignoring the tightening around his wrists. "Damien, I've spoken to your mother. She's worried sick about you. Think about your mother, kid. She doesn't know where you've gone off to. She doesn't know that you—that you chose this. To come here."

He was determined to tread carefully around this newly revived Damien, but the boy only stared at him and said, his face blank, "My mother would've been the first to die if I hadn't come to the Nocturnals. They told me something, you see. Something important."

"What did they tell you, Damien?"

"Oh, the kid's ears are filled with Infected shit," Hickory hissed. "I knew you were a cockhead, Cadshaw. Didn't realize you were gullible too. These monsters don't even *speak*." He twisted his neck and spat on the Nocturnal locking him in place. The figure didn't flinch, but the others in the circle shifted. Hickory laughed. "I forgot, though. You don't give a piss about whether they speak or not. You always *loved* them Nocturnals, didn't you, Cadshaw?"

I always loved a good shut-the-fuck-up, Joah thought furiously.

He locked eyes with Damien again.

"Listen, kid, can you communicate with them?" When the boy nodded, Joah said, "Okay. I believe you. Can you tell him —Prince Kal—that we don't mean any harm? He can keep the ax. We just want to bring you home. We're not built to live in the night," he added, glancing at Misla, who was sagging in her captor's incandescent arms.

"They can't let you go unless you promise to help," Damien whispered. The lantern's firelight was fading, but the prince Nocturnal's strange tattoos irradiated the boy's face. "They told *me*, but I can't do much about it. They only called my name because they were getting desperate and thought a kid might listen better than a grown-up. They thought I might convince you. *You* could stop it from happening. You could save my mother. And the rest of them too."

Joah paused for a heartbeat.

"Yes, okay," he said before Hickory could intervene. "What is it, then? What do they want to tell us?" In his mind, he heard his wife's Infected voice squeaking, *"Warn you. Got to. Warn, warn, warn,"* and his heart clogged with renewed fear.

Damien glanced up at Prince Kal. The Nocturnal didn't nod, but something unspoken seemed to pass between beast and boy's locked gaze.

"They'll tell you if you can prove your innocence," Damien said. "In a trial."

"Prove our—?"

"Innocence, yes. Your loyalty."

"And how the *fuck*," Hickory spat without warning, writhing in place again, "do you expect us to prove our goddamn *loyalty* to animals who can't *talk*? They're even uglier than the pictures back home. *Vultures* is what they are. Great big buzzards without wings."

Damien stared at him in silence. Joah decided not to break it. He had lost track of time, of how many cycles it had been since he'd first set out with Misla to warn the miners and scavengers about the early bells; daytime seemed like a distant, decaying memory now.

He was surprised, therefore, when the sky above seemed to shift with moving wisps of clouds and a sliver of the ice moon grinned down upon them. *The moon is king of the Eternal Night,* Joah thought weakly. He glanced at Misla again, and his stomach twisted.

He needed her to be okay.

"You said she'd be helped, Damien," Joah said desperately. The prince Nocturnal turned his violet eyes upon him with fierce curiosity. "Get Misla some help, and we'll do whatever we need to do. Tell us how to prove our loyalty."

An exhale passed through the ring of Nocturnals. Moonlight glinted off something in their hands, and for the first time in his bewildered state, Joah noticed they were all clutching identical, foot-long rods. Somehow, he knew the rods contained darts like the one that had killed Hickory's comrade: darts that might imbed themselves in his or Misla's skulls too.

Damien smiled.

"You'll have to learn their language first," he said.

"Learn their—?"

"Language, yes."

Joah had never believed in the Eternal Night before now. Nighttime lasted thirty years. Same as the day. It had always been so. Yet the darkness spreading through him when he understood what Damien was saying—*that* seemed eternal, like endless ribbons of curling black.

The Nocturnals wanted to Infect them. And Joah was supposed to let them.

They were forced down the High Road, their footsteps loud as they crunched and crackled over dead pine needles and twigs.

The Nocturnals, on the other hand, trod soundlessly. Their tattoos blazed like some absurd, glowing maze of rivulets. Joah stared at them as they ducked beneath overhanging branches. General Deckler had always described Nocturnal skin as dark and dense, all the better to blend in with the Eternal Night and sneak up on prey. But this conglomeration of patterns would scare prey *away*. It would also confuse—maybe even blind— nighttime predators.

Were the Nocturnals hunted by something worse than themselves?

He shook away this absurd curiosity and craned his neck for Misla. She was staggering along behind him, unbound but prodded in the spine whenever she faltered. Joah bit his tongue until he tasted the copper of his blood. He'd have to play his part perfectly, refrain from raising his voice at these voiceless creatures if he wanted to save Misla and escape.

Hickory, however, didn't seem to care about offending the Nocturnals. Up ahead, he was bellowing names at them, spitting at their bony backs, and laughing.

The Nocturnal clasping his elbow didn't react, but Damien turned widened eyes upon him every so often, and the prince kept shooting glances over his shoulder with narrowed violet slits. Again, something besides terror clogged Joah's throat—*embarrassment.* For some unshakeable reason, he didn't want these night monsters thinking humans were inferior. Yet one of them had already been caught mid-assault, and another was roaring songs like a madman.

Focus on Misla, Joah bade himself. *Just get Misla the hell out of here, then re-evaluate your idea of the Nocturnals. You can tell Deckler everything when you find sunlight again.*

Ahead, the High Road snaked its way into a cave. Joah blinked, swooning, on the verge of collapse. He was shell-shocked, he knew, maybe even hallucinating. The branches of pines had shot braided arms across the road, clasping hands with their counterparts on the other side. It formed a kind of knitted roof overhead. Like an upside-down nest.

Even Hickory quieted when the party prodded into its depths.

The Nocturnals, it seemed, had used this forest to build their temporary home—not by chopping the trees down, but by lacing them together using a glistening, rope-like material Joah had never seen before. The shining spirals of more Nocturnals lingered beyond the edge of the trees. Glowing dots peppered the ceiling, moving in lazy waves.

"Sunflies," Damien told him. "They carry little lights in their butts."

Joah jumped. He hadn't noticed the boy fall in step beside him. Most of the Nocturnals were drifting off into the forest to join the subtle movement of a hundred other bodies, but Damien and Prince Kal led Joah, Misla, Hickory, and their captors onward. The dwindling party stopped at a hulking contraption blocking the High Road like a giant metal toad. Beyond it, a tangle of material, like the extension of branches, formed a wall. The back of the cave.

"In here," Damien said.

They turned left before the contraption, into the spaces between trees. The braided ceiling continued overhead, blocking them from the moon's glaring grin. More violet eyes watched them pass, pausing mid-work. Some were chiseling stones that formed unfinished, indiscernible statues. Others were tending to pens of what looked horribly like hand-sized spiders: Joah watched a Nocturnal gathering strings of silk from a nest of webs before his captor jabbed him onward. Everywhere around them, those strange glistening ropes wrapped around groups of trunks, forming miniature caves or nests or...

Houses, Joah admitted, shivering. The monsters he had always feared didn't have a dozen eyes. They killed rapists with slender darts and made statues and lived in little woven houses.

Prince Kal led them to a trio of cage-like structures surrounded by even more watching Nocturnals. They were all roughly the same height, Joah noticed, and their heads glimmered in the light of the sunflies, inky from those sprouts of feathers. They didn't wear clothes, but their tattoos were *like* clothes, and Joah suddenly felt naked without designs imprinting his own skin.

"You'll stay here until you can hear them like I can," Damien said. "They'll bring you food and water and medicine, but you can't leave until you prove—"

"Our *innocence*. Yeah, yeah," Hickory spat. "Just call me roadkill already."

They were ushered into the cages. The metal around Joah's wrists snapped open with a small *click*. He buckled to his knees. The walls surrounding him were porous. He could see flakes of Misla as she collapsed too, and Hickory as he rammed a shoulder into his closed door.

The next few arcsecs blurred together.

Buckets of water met Joah's lips. Wooden bowls were shoved into his arms. Hot liquid was squirted up his nostrils. Joah's body relaxed as the pain floated off his shoulders. His ribs quit aching. His throat quit burning. He nearly inhaled an offering of chewy, rain-sized seeds, not knowing or caring where the Nocturnals had found them.

Eventually, the violet eyes dispersed. Damien and Prince Kal disappeared. Refusing to sleep just yet, Joah watched Misla through the holes in his wall. She had regained a flush of color, and somehow, the Nocturnals had repaired her clothes.

"Misla," he croaked.

She turned her head, but Hickory snorted before she could speak.

"Okay, Cadshaw, keep trying to woo my girl, why don't you? I know how this'll go. You've got some magic connection with the Nocturnals. Not that I think these crows *are* the Nocturnals—they don't look like the things that killed my grandpa when he was general—but *you* think they are. I can see it in your eyes. You'll find a way to woo them too, get on their good side, and then Misla will choose you over me. Yeah, I get it."

"I am *not* your girl, Hickory."

Misla hadn't uttered a single word since the appearance of the Nocturnals. Since her attacker had slumped dead upon her body. Now her voice dripped with smooth venom.

"Don't *ever* call me your girl again."

"Oh, c'mon, Misla. You know I love you. I'd do anything to—"

"You don't love me, Hickory. You hurt me."

A sunfly wandered into Joah's cage, carrying its own little speck of sunlight. Joah wrenched his eyes away from the mesmerizing light in time to see the pain contorting Misla's face. Hickory's next laugh shook with forced humor.

"I'd never hurt you, pretty girl. It's Cadshaw—it's *him* who'll hurt you."

"You wouldn't hurt me?" Misla whispered. "You wouldn't *hurt* me? Four years ago, you squeezed my ass in front of your friends and told them you'd like it a bit thicker."

"Well, you did thicken up, and now you look better than ever, so I was right, wasn't I?"

"You called me a whore," Misla said, that deadly voice raising an octave, "even though you were the one sleeping with other women. *Pretty girl. Whore. Pretty girl.* You used those little nicknames interchangeably."

"As if you didn't dream of sleeping with other men. I saw the way you looked at some of them. The way you looked at *Cadshaw* whenever he led the Infected back."

Joah wished he could rip Hickory's tongue from his throat. Stop the beast from mangling Misla more. But Misla was rising, curling her fingers through the holes in her cage.

"You talked me out of becoming a retriever again and again, and when I'd argue with you, you'd yell and grab my arms and shake me until I couldn't breathe."

"Retrievers don't do *shit*, Misla. They let the Nocturnals kill my grandfather. They're scams, every one of them. You wouldn't have taken me seriously without a little yelling or—"

"You killed a woman before General Deckler gave you permission."

"She was *Infected*. A lunatic! A danger to the community."

"You were going to rape me after you watched your friend do it first."

Hickory's mouth jutted open, but Joah cut through the inhale.

"Don't you dare try to make some pathetic, half-assed excuse for this one," he said, his old anger roiling inside him.

Misla sunk back into a crouch, hugging her knees to her chest. A chorus of buzzing had swelled around them, but her last, lethal whisper cut through this new noise like a blade.

"You have never refrained from hurting me before, Hickory. So why start now?"

The sunflies outside their prisons scattered at her words. Despite that roof plaited somewhere between forest floor and treetops, Joah felt the moon's descent, a release of pressure in the back of his skull. One cycle down in the Eternal Night. How many more to go?

"You know, Glade, you're right," he said. Through the gaps in his wall, he caught a flicker of movement as Hickory's head snapped up. "I *will* woo the Nocturnals. Misla and I *will* escape. And if you don't rot in this cage, if I ever see your free face again, I'll bury one of those sleek darts in your head. Just like what happened to your little friend."

He had hoped this last threat would crumble Hickory's façade, but his wife's killer just grinned, and Joah understood with a jolt: night monsters didn't have any friends to weep over.

Can you hear me, Joah?

Over the last countless cycles, Joah's eyes had become more and more adjusted to the darkness, until his surroundings looked slathered in gray film rather than an ink-black cloak. By the time the whiskers on his chin had grown into a nest of facial hair, he could make out the other animals haunting this enclosed forest space. There were swooping, flapping creatures Damien called *bats*. Coons slunk from tree to tree, and owls hooted from the crooks of their branches.

Reptiles with smooth, flexible bodies and centipede-like legs scuttled through the grass. Massive spiders caught hordes of sunflies in their sweeping webs.

Damien had been visiting their cages regularly to deliver more of those raindrop-sized seeds, along with heaps of nuts, roots, mushrooms, and cooked nettles. He'd tried teaching them the Nocturnal language by staring silently into their cells for arcsecs at a time.

"The brain's a mirror," he would say when Hickory only cussed and Misla and Joah stared blankly back. "Look into my eyes and find your own intentions reflected inside them. Only then will you be able to see beyond the mirror. That's what Prince Kal says, anyway."

They'd cough and stare. Damien would cluck his tongue, his bare feet, Joah noticed, digging into the dirt outside their doors, muddied toes burrowing deep.

"C'mon," the boy said once, "we're *close*. It's easier the closer you are. When you're far apart, it's like... it's like somebody's calling your name through the far end of a tunnel. Everything's dark and damp and squirming with bugs, and you've got no choice but to follow the echo to get to the light. But now we're at the end of the tunnel together. Look into my eyes."

Prince Kal always stood in the background, his willowy figure leaning into the crooks of trees, watching Damien teach. As nighttime deepened, tree trunks were shedding their bark like scabs, revealing fresh naked wood that oozed with interweaving streams of sap. Joah supposed it was a trick of his new night eyes, but those streams seemed to glisten, blending in with the coiling designs on the prince Nocturnal's inquisitive face.

After countless attempts to let the boy violate his brain, Joah had decided he simply wasn't capable of infection like his wife had been. He was immune.

Until now.

Can you hear me, Joah?

It was moontime. The forest buzzed and chirped and squawked and growled, as alive for the moon as daytime critters were awake for the sun. Joah had been lying sprawled on the ground. When Misla's voice whispered in his ear, he jumped, thinking she must have escaped and unlocked his prison door and slunk into his cage. But no. She was lying in *her* prison cell, her eyes peering through a hole in the twining wall separating them. Her lips weren't moving.

Joah. Can you hear me?

Those familiar goosebumps crawled up his neck. He wasn't sure how to respond.

I think I understand, Misla said.

Joah clapped a hand to his ear as if a sunfly had crawled inside, but her whispers were *inside* him, kneaded into his own thoughts.

The Nocturnals build these—oh, I don't know, these walls—whatever they're made of—to protect them from night beasts. But a long time ago, they must have been more exposed. And when you're exposed in the Eternal Night, making any kind of sound puts you on a pedestal. A dinner plate.

She blinked, and Joah saw the flicker of a memory that wasn't his: Misla clawing her way through the cotton trees, calling for Damien in terrified whispers.

Telepathy is safer during the Eternal Night, she said. *Invisible brain signals. Words without sound. Kind of like how flocks of migrating birds tell each other when to turn. Only more advanced.*

He stared into her eyes, let himself melt into their depths.

You've infected me, Misla, he thought. *God, this can't be real.*

It's not infection. It's connection. It's what we've been missing all along. Damien and your wife and all the others—they must've gone crazy because they were at the end of the long tunnel. But here, in the Eternal Night, we're closer to them. It's easier to hear and listen.

She paused.

I can hear you, Joah.

He had not meant to reveal his thoughts as he lost himself in the glow of her eyes, which had taken on a purple sheen. She was such a pure woman, no matter what had happened to her. She had a sharp mind, a soft heart. He thought back to her furious determination to save Damien in the conical tower, the way their bodies had cushioned the boy between them.

A tear pricked his inner eye.

I can hear you too, Misla.

For a long while, as Hickory snored in the cage beyond, they swapped their suspicions and plans voicelessly. They wouldn't try to fight. They would win the prince's approval, agree with whatever prompted the Nocturnals to lure their people into darkness.

And when the Nocturnals soften, Joah said, *we steal Damien and run.*

Misla nodded. Despite her insistence that it was telepathy, a tunnel-like connection forging their minds together, he kept thinking, *Infection isn't so bad, actually.* He thought of Blair, and his chin trembled with a smile: she hadn't died raging with fever, after all; she had died *bilingual*. His old anger seemed to sink below an exhausted horizon within him.

You're ready, then?

This was Damien. As the pressure of the moon descended, he had appeared noiselessly outside their cages. The Nocturnal prince lurked behind him. Joah blinked. The sap trickling down the deadened trees matched the bright purple veins intersecting Damien's Infected face. Both looked eerily similar to the designs clothing the prince's body, and Joah thought, *My God, is the Eternal Night just a maze of light?*

In a way, Damien replied, his eyes twinkling. *Come on, you two. As soon as Queen Usai heard the hum of your conversation, she had them set up the trial.*

Queen Usai. Another figurehead to contend with. Joah's mind burned as he focused on withholding his treacherous thoughts about escape. Prince Kal stepped forward and pressed a twisted stick of steel against the outside of their doors, which creaked open without prompting. Hickory stirred inside his cage, but by the time the ex-executioner had roused himself enough to shout insults through the cracks in his wall, Joah and Misla were already treading after Damien and

Prince Kal, boundless, weaving between bleeding trees.

"You Infected TRAITORS!" Hickory bellowed behind them.

Joah wondered if newfound veins were protruding from his *own* face, just as they had on Blair's and Damien's. He peeked at Misla, but though her cheeks were bright and flushed, her skin hadn't yet split like shattered eggshells.

Damien, Joah said, struggling to keep up with the prince's long strides and the boy's quick pit-pattering. Despite the medicine, his ribs still vaguely ached. *Where are we going?*

To the mountaintop. Damien brushed aside a brittle branch, which snapped and tumbled to the forest floor. Misla stumbled over it, and Joah caught her by the elbow.

The forest is dying, Misla said, her thoughts fringed with fear.

Not dying.

This newer, deeper voice spiked Joah's body with chills. Prince Kal did not turn from leading them through the enclosed forest, which was conspicuously empty of both Nocturnals and other night creatures.

Shedding, the prince said. *You see, the trees cannot Move like you or me. They are not nomads. They are not anchored to a segment of daytime like your people.*

They simply have two skins. One for your sun, and one for my moon.

Joah knew the vegetation couldn't possibly survive lack of sunlight for much longer, but he didn't want to cross with this foreboding creature picking his way through the woods ahead of them. He fought the urge to grab Damien's arm and run right then and there. It would do no good, he knew. His full strength had not yet returned, and they were still trapped inside this strange, nest-like cave.

In a haste to muffle his thoughts, Joah barked in their normal tongue, "Hey kid. Do you think—if Misla and I win this trial—you could have them give us some toilets? We've been having to shit in those empty water buckets, and I'm gagging myself to sleep every cycle."

Damien giggled.

"They thought the stench might motivate you to find your inner tongue more quickly. We don't have much time, you know. The clock's ticking."

Joah glanced at his own broken wristwatch as the forest floor began sloping upward. They panted as they climbed. The ground became jumbled with rock, and the ceiling above their heads began to fray, revealing pores like in their prison walls.

Eventually, when they had scrambled kilometers upward, the trees thinned and a light layer of snow dappled the ground. Roped ends of the Nocturnal-made walls had been staked to the dirt. The opening yawned like the mouth of a cave.

Or the end of a tunnel, Misla told him.

Cold air blasted their faces. At the same time, Joah's eyes seared with a sudden light. For a moment, he thought the Nocturnals had mounted the moon, but then his mouth fell open.

They were on a flat expanse of snow-laden rock, where a hundred Nocturnals sat in a circle on portable rounded chairs. Their designs glistened, and the snow gleamed, but neither were a match for the sky: despite the ice moon's absence, thousands—no, *millions*—of burning dots speckled the air above them, like a horde of sunflies too far to reach.

They are suns, Prince Kal said, finally turning to face them. The rest of the Nocturnals remained breathlessly silent, but they had all twisted their heads to watch Joah and Misla's entrance: two hundred violet eyes piercing their faces.

Suns? Misla gasped.

Faraway suns, Prince Kal said, giving the faintest nod. *We call them stars.*

He led them toward the circle of Nocturnals and four vacant chairs half-submerged in mounds of snow. An insistent buzzing rose as they drew nearer. Joah craned his neck for signs of new bugs or animals, but Damien nudged him and whispered, "It's the hum of conversation. Like the rumble of voices during recess or an execution."

Prince Kal nodded at the chairs, which were draped with sheeny cloaks that looked as if they were made of spider silk. Damien grabbed his and wrapped it around himself. Joah and Misla donned theirs too, then sank into spongy seats, shivering and looking around.

All eyes flickered toward the Nocturnal sitting at the head of the circle. Strings of teeth-like objects dangled from the sides of her head, where ears would have been if she'd had ears. Her designs, unlike the smoke-like spirals on Prince Kal, resembled a tangled mess of aged flowers—wrinkled circles ringing bigger circles. Wispy feathers stuck from her head like hair.

Queen Usai, Misla told Joah with a brief widening of her eyes.

Welcome to your trial, Joah Cadshaw and Misla Crane, the queen said, her thoughts booming over all the others. The buzzing quieted. *I was sad to hear of the other one's refusal to learn our ways. It was the only way this trial could commence. You see, our tongues are not made for verbal speech. Your people, however, possess the ability to receive our signals. When you are close to us, you can transmit those signals too.*

As she spoke, a few Nocturnals stalked away from the ring, crouching low over the mounds of snow surrounding them. They fiddled with something buried in the cold. After a series of *pops*, flames burst into being, encircling them in a loop of fire and heat. Joah squinted at the bonfire roots. He couldn't see wood or coal. It was as if the flames were feeding on snow.

Our light scares most monsters away, Queen Usai said as the fire-starters swept back to their seats. *But we still need extra protection from the Old Aro Calic. Our hunter. And in addition to the fire, you mustn't speak out loud. The Calic has excellent hearing.*

Joah felt that tingle of curiosity again, a zip of fear mingled with it. He was sitting among his own enemies, yet it seemed as though an even greater danger prowled the night.

Indeed, Queen Usai mused. *Now, I am going to ask the two of you some questions. It is much harder to suppress your thoughts in open spaces such as these, so being truthful shouldn't be too hard of a feat. I have been trying for nearly sixty years, you see, to contact your people, to warn you of the dangers ahead. But I do not know whom to trust.*

We are yours to ask, Your Highness, Misla sent, bowing her head. A grumble of voiceless laughter rippled around the ring. Queen Usai pulled back her lipless mouth in a smile.

Very well. We'll start with you, Misla Crane. Our young friend here tells me that you report to a certain Aoif Deckler. Is this true?

It is, said Misla, glancing at Joah uncertainly. He gave her a nod, his heart pounding.

And why would you want to work for such a man? It seems he orders you to abduct what your people call "the Infected". He teaches you how to kill us, in the case that we ever—

Joah couldn't help himself. It was much easier to chew his tongue than to withhold the roar of thoughts in his chest, especially, for some reason, under the vast spread of stars.

It's not abduction to bring back the abducted. Your Highness, he added. *It's rescue.*

Queen Usai's earrings tinkled in the silence. The fire swaying behind her made Joah's eyes ache. He looked up at the strew of stars overhead instead.

The people we make contact with have always chosen *to come to us,* Prince Kal growled when the queen remained silent.

Is that right? Joah asked, a heated panic rising within him. Sweat tickled his forehead. *So you think my wife—one night she wants a baby, and the next she'd rather leave me and her own home and the goddamned sun to hang out with a bunch of night monsters?*

Misla shot him an alarmed glare. Queen Usai stroked her chin.

If I am not much mistaken, she said, *your wife was Blair Cadshaw. Our people do not own two names, but I can see the practicality of joining a second one when you find a mate.*

Joah shook in his chair. Misla's hand slipped into his and squeezed his fingers.

Yes, your wife was Blair, the queen continued. *I can taste your grief over her loss, so I will excuse your outburst. Grief can strangle us for so many years. But may I remind you that it was not we who killed her. In fact, we never met her. Right before she reached us, she was snatched away.* The queen peered into Joah's eyes, the violet of her own reeling his gaze away from the stars. *Your wife chose to come to us, just as Damien here chose to come to us. We have made contact with others in your community, you see, who refused to come, who shook it off as a bad dream. More refused than accepted. We always respected their decision to stay.*

Joah shook his head. If this was true, Blair would have chosen to stay too.

Blair thought she could make Aoif Deckler listen, Prince Kal said. *Because she was mated with you. One of the general's best retrievers. She chose to find us, to get closer so that she could hear the full extent of our message. The closer she got, the more she understood. She knew the gist of it by the time you found her, but the further you hauled her away, the less she could communicate her findings. It's hard for your kind to access our language from a distance.*

Joah could taste the accusation in Prince Kal's tone. He gripped Misla's fingers, their palms slipping with sweat. The irony of this situation seared him: *he* was being accused of kidnapping his own wife. He almost laughed.

You are not being accused of anything just yet, Queen Usai said. The thoughts of the other Nocturnals buzzed around them for a flickering moment. *I want to know why both of you chose to work for Aoif Deckler. It is not your actions that matter here. It is your intentions.*

To Joah's left, Damien nodded pointedly at Misla, his warning like a faint breeze. Misla cleared her throat. The Nocturnals around her recoiled from the sound.

I can't speak for my partner here, she said, *but I wanted to talk to the Infected— the bilingual, if you will—to find out what made them leave their homes. I've always been horrified that we behead the Infected when we bring them back. I wanted to change things.*

The truth of her words shivered around the ring. The fire flared. Joah's mind bounced back to their conversation right before they had met the scavengers. He hoped the Nocturnals could access this memory to verify Misla's authenticity. Maybe *she* could escape with Damien, even if they threw Joah back into the twisted prison cells next to Hickory.

And what of you, Joah Cadshaw? Queen Usai asked after a crackling moment of silence. *Why did you become a retriever?*

Joah glanced at Misla, who nodded encouragingly. He swallowed.

Well, my granddad was a retriever. Even as he thought it, he knew this was not enough. He closed his eyes, allowed himself to sink into a cavernous honesty that he had never voiced aloud. *It's easy to believe in a day and night, okay? A darkness and a light. After I was fired— after my wife was killed—they put me in a community position. I had to catch the beasts living among us. It was much harder, because they all wore the same faces. But when you're a retriever, it feels good to pinpoint the monsters so easily. I was saving people from darkness.*

He paused.

I didn't know the Eternal Night could contain so much light. I didn't know you glowed.

The firelight was dropping, but those far-off suns winked above them.

I see, Queen Usai said eventually. *Ignorance, then. Not malevolence. What do you think, Damien?*

Damien twisted in his seat to tilt his head at Joah and Misla.

"Will you save my mom if they tell you?" His voice trembled.

"Of course, kid," Joah said automatically. "Of course we'll save your mom."

Damien turned back to the queen and nodded. Queen Usai made a peculiar twirling motion with her fingers, and a deep buzzing drowned out the sounds of popping fire. It became a roar of sound, like blood was thundering through Joah's ears.

Queen Usai dropped her hands. The roar smothered itself into silence.

Very well. I will tell you. I can see now that you didn't know... couldn't possibly have foreseen. Of course you'd think of us as monsters. But you have to abandon that notion now. You must promise to save your people from the darkness, not behind them, but ahead of them.

Yes, Joah and Misla said together, still holding slippery hands.

Good, Queen Usai said. *Here it is, then, what I have been trying to tell your people for nearly sixty years: there is no fissure ahead of you. The High Road remains unbroken.*

No, Joah said. Warning bells clanged in his memory. He saw Aoif's boxy figure bending over the map, his finger touching that vicious red slash. *General Deckler said the scouts—*

Did you talk to the scouts yourselves? Prince Kal asked. *Did you see the fissure with your own eyes? Or did your people jolt into emergency status at the word of one man?*

Joah flinched, but the Nocturnal queen plunged on before he could answer.

I knew Aoif Deckler sixty years ago, when he was a gangly teenager. I know him better than you do. She paused, her earrings rattling ominously. *I know the man still. So trust me when I tell you: the imposter has been planning this since he helped murder your previous general. He is not leading your community to safety. He is leading you straight into a trap.*

And Joah could sense the queen's genuine terror, and he felt Damien tremble beside him, and Misla's fingernails pierced the back of his hands as the dying fire spit feeble sparks into that everlasting night air, and he knew the Nocturnals were right.

Warn you. Got to, Blair's ghost sang in his head.

General Deckler was sending the Sunsetters to their graves.

Night

Prince Kal closed his eyes to avoid watching the anguish crumple the alien's face.

He poured forth his memories instead, allowing the foreign guests to access his wordless thoughts, all the sights and sounds and smells of a cruel cycle sixty years ago, when he had just reached manhood. Back before they were forced to Move.

It was finally sunset. His people had been hiding from the scorching heat of daytime for thirty years, unable to step outside, forced to hunker in the shadows of their towers. Kal had never seen the moon; it was always washed out by sunlight, a faint white halo among the clouds. Oh, he had dreamed about it, though, that piercing disk pinned to its black curtain of night sky.

Now the beastly sun was actually sinking into a bloodred grave over the sea, and twilight would soon sweep over them, and he'd be able to bask in the moon's pool of light at last.

Kal.

It was his mother. He had been squinting through the window in a turret on the fourth floor, watching the rays of sunset stroke the dappled water; he jumped when she swept around the corner. The queen was swaddled in her usual silk cloak that would shield her if she were to accidentally stumble into sunlight. Kal had thought she'd scold him for exposing himself at the window, but her thoughts were harried, choked.

Kal, come with me. There is a commotion in the Grand Hall. It seems a Diurnal has snuck into the castle. I want you close to me, in case there are more.

Not a sunman. A Diurnal. One of those strange people who, despite their name, followed sunrise or sunset religiously, Moving every few years to avoid the heat of day and terrors of night.

Prince Kal wrapped his cloak tight around his body and raced after his mother, through the twisting halls where firelight flickered from steel brackets. They cut across the indoor courtyard, past the tinkling fountain, and eased open the doors of the Grand Hall together.

Nobody noticed them. Their cloaks blended into the shadows, but King Isce and his guardsmen had taken their own off; the glowing patterns on their skin highlighted the alien-looking creature screaming and writhing in their midst.

Reddish mops sprouted from the Diurnal's head, and strangely muted clothes hugged the curves of his body. His ears were large, ugly, and crimped, sticking out from the side of his face. Nothing about him glowed.

You have broken into our domain. Killed two of my sentries, Kal's father snarled. He was sprawled in his usual spiked stone chair, unflinching, though his patterns flared. *Why?*

I know what you do to my people, the Diurnal hissed, trying to wrench himself from the grips of the guards. *I know how you—how you... infect them! You lure them away.*

Beside Kal, Queen Usai's thoughts fluttered in alarm, but she didn't let them extend beyond their bubble hidden in shadows. Kal knew why she was afraid, though—the Diurnal knew their language, had unleashed his thoughts as if he were a native. They, on the other hand, had never been able to make those peculiar sounds of speech the Diurnals practiced.

Well, said the prisoner, *I followed some of them, followed them away from the High Road, all the way here. It took them twenty cycles just to reach your fortress. Clever, making your food prance to you instead of catching them yourself. You don't even have to leave your roost.*

Now Prince Kal and the queen passed confusion, though Kal sensed dread lacing his mother's thoughts. Food? What did the alien mean, food? The sunmen brought them carcasses to eat during the day, when they couldn't afford to step outside, and during the Eternal Night they scavenged for carrion themselves, but when had they ever lured —?

A screech from behind him. Kal ducked as a great horned owl swooped through the cracked doorway and landed with a *flump* on King Isce's patterned shoulder. The owl shook its body—feathers floated outward—and wretched: the corpse of a vole, slimed with mucus and blood, poured onto King Isce's naked lap.

Lowering his head, the king extended his spiked tongue, wrapped it around the vole, and reeled it into his mouth. When the owl took off again with another screech, King Isce extended his hands, as if to say, *See?*

That's not what I mean, pouted the alien. *You don't just lure owls.*

The king laughed before Kal could form any kind of half-baked conclusion. Air puffed in quick waves from his lips, and humor riddled his next words.

Fine. You've caught me, Diurnal. I have my ancestor's taste, I will admit. When your people wander past us so willingly, just within reach... when I can sense the abilities some possess, the abilities to understand us, to answer our calls... but why have you come here, Diurnal? Have you come to scold me for my choice in dessert?

Queen Usai gripped her son's elbow, her nails piercing his skin. She tried to pull him away, back through the doors and away from the truth, but he wrenched himself from her grip. He stared at his father. He had never loved the man, but... would he really prey upon *Diurnals*? *Living* Diurnals, nonetheless? Walking, *talking* Diurnals?

I have come, the alien panted, *to offer you a deal.*

The Grand Hall silenced. Kal and his mother stiffened in their efforts to close their minds, to not make a sound. King Isce leaned forward.

A deal? What could you possibly offer me that—?

A year ago, my mother got sick, said the Diurnal. *I met with our general, begged him to send scavengers to find some medicine. He's the one with the authority to make those decisions, you know. He met with me, alright. Told me he couldn't help me. Said he needed to use the scouts and scavengers to find more* ship *supplies, or else we wouldn't have enough vessels to take everyone across the Green Sea when the Eternal Night comes. And my mother died.*

King Isce stroked his jawline, where one of his glowing designs angled crookedly from a scar. *I don't understand what this has to do with me. What do I care if a nomad dies?*

He chose the Dirt Slummers over my mother, said the alien. *The Dirt Slummers! They squabble and fuck and overpopulate, and he chose* them. *Meanwhile, my mother was a prominent member of the community. An inventor. She created the magnetic watch strapped to General Glade's own damn wrist, but he let her die! No, he should've left the Slummers behind, abandoned them to the Eternal Night like he abandoned her.*

King Isce said nothing. Blood still smothered his lips. Kal tried to control his shuddering breaths. He thought of their castle cellar, piled high with the bones of rodents and sometimes even mammals. Were there *other* creatures trapped inside? Creatures with mops of hair and crimped ears and plain skin that his father had lured from the High Road over yonder?

Help me overcome General Glade, the alien said. *Help me take the general's place, and you can have all the piss-poor schmucks you want. No need to lure them. I'll give them to you. You can lock them in that cellar of yours, let them rot to the ripeness of your liking. Help me fight, and I promise—in sixty years, when the poorest, dirtiest of us have squabbled and fucked and overpopulated again, I'll give you them again. And again, and again, for as long as I live, for as long as my children lead in my place. Help me kill our general, and you've got yourself a feast.*

Now Queen Usai's nails sunk deep into her son's arms; blood oozed from the curved indents, like a trickling frown. This time, Kal let her tug him backward, but not before he heard his father ask, *What's your name, son?*

And the alien replied, *Aoif Deckler, Your Highness.*

☽

How long had Joah known General Deckler? Since he was a boy, as young as Damien, and his school had hosted a career day where all the professionals—miners, healers, scouts, scavengers—had ringed their wheeled gymnasium, thrusting out fliers that said things like:

THANK YOUR LOCAL WARNER.

COME DE-STRESS WITH A SEAMSTRESS.

A NOMADIC PLUMBER'S GUIDE

When General Aoif Deckler himself had walked into the room, his hair already salted with white, the students had *oooh*'d and *ahhhh*'d, turning away from their current interests. Joah remembered straightening in his crisp school uniform, breathless as he watched the general march to the center of the gymnasium and hold out a neat stack of business cards. His classmates had streamed around the man, and by the time Joah got to him, there were no business cards left.

"Ahh, you're too late, sonny," General Deckler had said, chuckling. "Well, that's okay. I've got in *here*," he said, pulling another, smaller card from his inside pocket, "my *real* contact info.

Can't have all you little tykes sending letters to my office, can I?"

"No, sir," Joah had said, taking this newer card with delicate, trembling fingers.

"No, indeed. Say, you've ever thought of being a retriever?"

"My granddad was one, sir. But he retired before he crossed the Green Sea."

"Your granddad! Tell me, what was his name? I must know..."

So it had begun: Joah's relationship with the man he had come to trust, the man he'd always admired even after he'd been fired. Yet he could not deny the sincerity of Prince Kal's memories. Nocturnals could withhold, but they could not, Joah had learned, so blatantly lie.

His chair seemed to sink deeper into the snow. The fire ringing them had dwindled to embers, and the cold of the mountaintop bit his body with frosted teeth. To his right, Misla was looking up at the stars, as if hoping to find an answer etched somewhere in the aro sky. To his left, Damien's fingers fidgeted on his lap, and now Joah knew what the boy had meant when he had said *"My mother would've been the first to die if I hadn't come to the Nocturnals."*

Damien's mother was a Dirt Slummer.

After witnessing what happened in the Grand Hall, Queen Usai said now, using her voiceless speech like thoughts sent along a cold gale, *my son and I snuck to the cellar. There, we found a handful of Diurnals... decomposing among the skeletons of other creatures.*

She seemed to sense the lingering question rising, smoke-like, from Joah and Misla's tilted heads: why let them decay? Of course, Joah thought he knew the answer, but it made him feel sick, and he wondered if he'd ever be able to stomach meat again. Maybe he'd eat those raindrop-sized seeds for the rest of his life.

We cannot digest fresh produce or flesh like you do. We eat what is abandoned by the sun. Although the land and its vegetation doesn't die during the Eternal Night, there are enough plants and animals that do. We clean it all up, so to speak.

Joah thought back to that mysterious tower at sunset. At the bone fragments crunching beneath his feet. Then he thought of the seeds again, seeds that had also been left behind by whatever squirrely creature had hoarded them. The Nocturnals were, in the truest sense of the word, scavengers. They were not predators. Yet King Isce had obviously accepted General Deckler's offer. He had agreed to hunt and capture and kill.

And now, sixty years later, he was about to do it again.

"You've been infecting us all this time," Joah said aloud, "to warn us of an upcoming massacre? A massacre like the one before?"

He realized his mistake when Misla inhaled sharply and the Nocturnals made a collective twitching motion, as if the sound from his lips had struck them with a spark of electricity: there was a reason the Nocturnals didn't make noise outside their protective netted cave. In the Eternal Night, when light and sight were scarce, sound exposed you to the monsters lurking in shadows.

They all waited, breathless, for something to happen, but there was only the creak of trees and snapping of branches in the distance as the wind broke into a howl.

I'm sorry, he said. *I forgot. I*—he was so shocked at what he had learned that his thoughts had turned into speech. The beasts they'd thought of as ever-evasive ghosts, always trailing them, always hypnotizing and luring their people into the darkness, had only been trying to stop them from the real darkness that waited for them at the Green Sea like an open jaw.

I never loved my husband, Queen Usai said, her sharp-angled shoulders relaxing slightly in the absence of a night beast. *It was an arranged partnership. When we saw what he had agreed to, I begged him to reconsider, but...*

A yowl cut through her words like a bloody ax.

The surrounding Nocturnals jumped from their seats, the feathers on their skulls bristling. Damien sprang to his feet too, and Joah saw the glint of a pole clasped in his small, muddied hand. The embers had died. Through the last torrents of steam rising from the snow, a curled set of horns bobbed over the mountain's edge.

The Calic, Queen Usai moaned.

A massive reptilian cat prowled into view. Scales covered its sleek body, and horns protruded from its jawline, curving upward like spiked ears. Its tail whipped behind it like a snake. Its eyes, each the size of Joah's palm, glared at the mountaintop party with slanted fury.

Queen Usai opened her lipless mouth and made a strange screeching noise. It was far more terrifying than if she had screamed instruction inside her own head: it was the rickety, rusty howl of a throat that never got used unless the enemy was already upon them.

The Nocturnals flew together, forming a tight knot within the circle of chairs. Joah grabbed Misla and Damien and pulled them into the tangle of limbs. The Nocturnals' glowing designs burned orange, and when they started swaying in unison, their mass of bodies waved like open flame. Joah was reminded, suddenly, of the mass of birds that had attacked him and Misla on the High Road on their way to retrieve those who had been left behind.

The night beast paused. Its lips curled backward, revealing a clutter of yellow, needle-like teeth. Mid-sway, the Nocturnals pulled out those identical poles, and the mountaintop roared and crashed with waves of that rising sound: a cacophony of grinding screeches from a hundred unused throats. They were trying to scare the beast away.

Damien slipped from Joah's grip and ducked under a Nocturnal's legs.

"Hey, kid!" Joah called, reaching out for him, but his hand was slapped away by an elbow, and Damien had already disappeared in the thickness of fiery bodies. "Come back!"

His voice was lost in the screeching discord. The boy had weaseled his way out of the fireball and now stood, exposed and alone, in the monster's warped shadow. His pole tumbled from his fingers into the snow. Compared to the crouching cat, Damien was nothing but a rodent. A single one of those curved claws would impale his chest like a sword.

What are you doing, child? Queen Usai cried.

Let me talk to him. I always wanted a cat, came Damien's voice, and the roar plummeted like an arrow arcing to the ground. The swaying stopped as everyone watched.

Joah saw himself, as if through a ghost's memory, picking up that green strip of fabric in the High Road's collection of dirt. Only now it was Damien Fertheli reaching a palm toward the cat, and Joah heard Lupita's sniveling voice as clearly as if she stood beside him now: *"He loves how wild they are, but I—I always told him no. I shouldn't have told him no,"* and Joah didn't have time to break from the Nocturnal huddle.

The cat leapt forward in a high arc, claws extended.

The Nocturnals moved in unison: left hands clutching the front of their poles, right hands gripping the back, they twisted each half in opposite directions as if unscrewing a lid.

Darts shot from their weapons like flaming arrows. Most *ping*'d against the cat's shelled skin, but two found its eyes, another its gaping mouth, and the beast shrieked in midair.

A flash of movement. Damien flew sideways as one of the Nocturnals, a slender one with dotted skin patterns, shoved him out of the way. The cat landed with a harrowing *THUMP* on top of the Nocturnal, right where Damien had been standing moments before.

Its serpentine tail kept thrashing for what felt like forever, its eyes blinking palm-sized beads of blood into the snow. Joah and Misla unglued themselves from the jumble of bodies and raced toward Damien, wrenching him backward. Frost had actually formed on the boy's eyelashes where tears would have clung. His lips had turned blue, and his fingers felt like icicles.

As the Nocturnals streamed around them to move the beast off their friend, Joah caught Misla's eye. Their breath fogged out in front of them, merging in midair above Damien's stiffened hair. Joah didn't need the Nocturnal language to understand the shine in Misla's eyes.

We need to go home, she was saying. *We need to save our people.*

Back within the humidity and warmth of the netted forest, they buried the Nocturnal who had saved Damien along with the parts of the Calic that had crushed him: a claw ripped from the paw, scales sawed from the chest, a strip of leathery skin from its chin. The rest of the beast had been picked apart to be eaten or used in other ways, to respect the beast itself, Queen Usai said, and in honor of the Nocturnal it had killed. The Nocturnal would live on in the blood they used for paint or the sinews that they would strip and use to make baskets, blankets, and bags.

His name was Gritz, Prince Kal told them as they watched Queen Usai herself push dirt into the grave, using one of the Calic's femurs like a shovel. They were only a few paces from the cages Joah and Misla had been living in, where the soil was loose and moist. Beyond Queen Usai's shoulder, Hickory Glade had crawled to the door of his own cage and pressed his face against the twining fibermud that contained him, watching her cover the grave.

Damien was standing rigid as a bone, staring at the patches of the

Nocturnal's face still visible beneath the clods of dirt, at the dots on his skin that had faded like cold coals. Joah could hear the horrified whispers inside the boy's head—he had not meant to get anyone killed. He had only meant to tame the great cat, to ride the Calic to dawn so he could save his mother.

Because Damien's mother, along with the rest of the Dirt Slummers, was in danger.

"It was a good idea, kid," Joah whispered, clapping a hand on the boy's shoulder. "But we're going to have to find another way to reach the Green Sea in time. Maybe the river…"

Even as he said it, he knew the river wasn't fast or strong enough to carry them, even on a boat, to the point where the sun would still be winking on the horizon. How many moon cycles had they been stuck here? Twenty? Thirty? Joah had lost count, but he knew it might be too late.

Queen Usai straightened from her shoveling, her earrings clinking.

There is a way to get to your people in time. I am sure they have yet to reach the Green Sea, though they will soon, much too soon. If you can just get fuel for the Shooting Star…

"Shooting Star?" Joah asked. "What do you mean, Shooting Star?"

At his mother's nod, Prince Kal conjured an image of that strange contraption at the back of their netted cave, squatting in the middle of the High Road like a fat metal toad. A machine. The Nocturnal version of a silver steed. But instead of wheeling across the landscape, it...

Flies, Prince Kal confirmed with a nod. *We didn't make them. My father found them long ago, a dozen of them, half-buried in rocks near the Green Sea. He said they looked like fallen metal stars. He spent years trying to figure out what might power it, but nothing worked... until a sunman—what your kind call a Leather Skin—told him to try the very thing the sun people suck from the stems of perennial trees. The sunmen were our slaves, you see,* Prince Kal added, his forehead wrinkled with shame. *They brought us carrion during the daytime. And supplies.*

He paused.

They were the ones who killed so many of your people for my father and Aoif Deckler.

Joah jolted. Leather Skins had always seemed the opposite of a Nocturnal. They were like far-off sun gods, epitomes of light, fighters of night. To imagine them as slaves, forced to murder and drag bodies back to their master, was like trying to imagine the moon swallowing the sun.

Yes, the moon does occasionally swallow the sun, Prince Kal said with a wry twist of his lipless mouth. *There are other communities of Nocturnals and Leather Skins, you know. Some choose to Move every thirty years. Some choose to Stay and hide from the heat of the day or dangers of night. My father chose the latter. He built our fortress on the edge of the Green Sea where he'd found the starships. But every thirty years, when daytime kept us in our towers, the nomadic Leather Skins would come around. And he would enslave them.*

"How?" Misla asked. "How could he even *get* to them, let alone enslave—?"

Some could communicate with us just like you are communicating with us now. My father used our language to lure them, to overpower them, to cripple them and force them into servitude. And they—the slaves—gave us the secret to the Shooting Stars, the fuel we needed to ignite the machines and travel the aro faster than the moon can rise and fall. The fuel was too bright and hot for us to touch, but the Leather Skins could gather it for us...

And now Joah heard a new word flutter from Prince Kal's mind like a single moth. But it was a word that somehow snapped the pieces—the mystery of the Eternal Night—together.

Sunsap.

It's what the trees and other perennial vegetation of the aro hoard in order to survive the thirty-year night, Queen Usai said, pausing in her efforts to fold Gritz within the aro's eternal embrace. *They collect excess energy from the sun, convert it to sap, and store it in an underground vault where it flows like a river from one forest to the next.*

Joah imagined a horde of roots wiggling beneath the aro, reaching for a steaming liquid that ran like golden blood through the veins of the aro.

And this same sap can be used to fuel the Shooting Stars, Queen Usai said. *When he discovered this, my husband sent some Leather Skins to mine more of it a few hundred kilometers out west. This was about a decade before Aoif Deckler approached him with the deal of a lifetime.* Her thoughts oozed sarcasm, and Joah briefly wondered how long a Nocturnal lifetime really *was.* Longer than his, by God. *Ironically, the largest sunsap reserve runs alongside your High Road. A good latitude, I assume. I believe you're already familiar with the access point?*

Within the aged, streaked mirror of her mind, Joah saw that strange conical tower again. Only now he understood what it was for: an entrance to a tunnel that led to the very thing keeping the aro alive during the Eternal Night. The thing Leather Skins consumed. The thing that would have fueled King Isce's flight across the sky. Because if there were other communities of Nocturnals, of *course* a tyrant like Isce would have wanted to soar over the rest of them. To dominate the world. To ascend in a way his wingless body never could.

To reach the moon.

"We need to mine the sunsap, don't we?" Misla said after a lengthy stretch of silence, in which Queen Usai resumed shoveling dirt into the grave at her feet. "You have a Shooting Star, but you don't have fuel. We need to fill the tank, so to speak."

Queen Usai bowed her head so low, she looked in danger of toppling into the half-filled hole. She steadied herself by spearing the aro with the curved edge of the Calic bone.

The starship we have with us now— Kal and I stole it and used it to fly after your general about a year after the Leather

Skins dragged all those corpses to our cellar. This was long after the sun had gone down, when it was safe for us to do so. When we finally touched down on the other side, we'd caught up to sunset again, and our tank was near empty. We've been dragging the starship with us for the last sixty years, but I do believe it would still work. If you want to save your people from this—Queen Usai brought the femur bone to her lips; her tongue shot out and spiraled around it like King Isce's had in Kal's memory—*you're going to have to gather sunsap, yes.*

"We're not Leather Skins, though," Misla said. "What if it burns us?"

Queen Usai smiled.

I have no doubt that bathing in the stuff might kill you, she said. *I would be careful not to touch it. But your bodies can withstand direct sunlight whereas ours can't, so I'm quite certain you'd be able to go near it, to collect it as carefully as you'd gather fire.*

There came a laugh from behind her, high-pitched, yet guttural. Hickory's eyes glimmered at them from within his cage, and Joah saw his grimy face splinter into a grin.

"You're not miners! This sunsap thing you mentioned, or whatever the hell it is... you think it's as easy as skipping down a tunnel and cuddling the stuff to your chest? No. You don't know a thing about caves." Hickory's eyes targeted Joah, and they glowered at each other with the pin-straight ferocity of shooting darts. "*You* didn't even know what a damn lantern was. You'll never make it without the light of the moon or these wretched flies buzzing around."

Joah glanced at Misla. For the first time in three cycles, he let himself remember Hickory standing over her again, berating her, laughing... he let himself remember the squishing slice of Hickory's ax through his wife's neck. His chest squeezed from the injustice of it all. How fitting, how perfectly goddamned ironic: they needed a miner to save their community in time.

But no, there had to be another way. He squinted at the pieces of Hickory he could see through the fibermud walls. "What's down there, then? What's in these caves you know so well? Tell us what to watch out for."

Hickory laughed again, his fingers curling around the ropes of his wall.

"Well, sometimes there's no good air to breathe. You'd never know until it's too late and you're choking on the gases of underground. Sometimes the walls come crashing down around you. It's never happened to me, because *I* know which signs of weakness to look for, but oh, it's happened plenty of times to others." His smile widened. "Sometimes there are creatures. Giant insects the size of a dog. Snakes and spiders and scorpions."

Damien's tiny chest rose and fell in awe struck breaths as Hickory continued describing the monsters that might or might not stop them from accessing the fuel they needed. Joah could feel the boy's thrill and eagerness, like a rapid heartbeat drumming up his neck, and he remembered the old Dirt Slummer's words from so long ago: *Damien liked to dig.* Yes, he did. And Damien would beg to come with them. In truth, Joah wasn't willing to separate from the boy until they returned to sunset and saw him safely in his mother's arms.

Was he willing, then, to lead the child into the unknown, without a guide to protect them from the beasts lurking underground? Beside him, Misla bit her lower lip and shook her head.

"I can help you," Hickory said now, the faintest crinkle of earnestness replacing those creases of his manic grin for the first time. "Let me out, and I'll help you find this... this sunsap. I just want to get out of his ruddy cage. I want to see the light again. Please."

Joah looked at Queen Usai, who shifted the last piles of dirt overtop Gritz's grave. Her blue-black feathers lay flat against her skull as if wilting. She set the femur bone at her feet.

To free your people, she said, *sometimes you need to free your monsters too.*

Prince Kal led them back toward the High Road, the glow of his figure swaying like a condensed sky of stars. Joah followed with tight unease, clutching a dart-loaded rod that Queen Usai had lent him. Misla marched beside him with Hickory's ax in one hand and his old lantern flickering in the other. Hickory glared at those hands as he slouched after them, his own locked behind his back with the snakish metal that had once handcuffed Joah too.

Damien—bless the kid—ignored their tension. He skipped around the peeling trees and hummed school tunes, inspiring a good number of Nocturnals to peek from their braided houses with hawkish eyes. Their thoughts of farewell rang in Joah's mind like Moving bells.

Yes, finally; they were Moving again.

"Hey, Prince," he said when the High Road finally appeared between trees. They weaved their way to the Shooting Star contraption squatting upon it near the back of the cave, and he asked his next question voicelessly, so that Hickory wouldn't hear. *Why do you call us aliens?*

Kal stared at the sunflies haloing the starship's metal head like a fiery crown.

You call us monsters, he said hesitantly, *but we have our own beliefs about your people. That you aren't native to the aro. That you came from the sky in a hundred starships centuries ago, and have since abandoned those starships. That you've forgotten where your people come from. I mean,* he added, *the Leather Skins can thrive in any time of day—all 180 degrees. We can flourish during all shades of night. But you—you're bound to a small, twelve-degree section of evening. Your bodies weren't built for such a fluctuation in light and heat. It's as if you weren't made for this planet. As if you really are aliens.*

The prince scrutinized them, ripping his gaze from the lifeless starship. They were all wearing silk cloaks to protect them from the bite of a cold night once they left the netted cave. Joah and Misla also shouldered supple, stretchy bags filled with dozens of ceramic jugs that they would fill with sunsap when they reached the vault beneath the conical tower.

"Why?" Joah asked suddenly, his thoughts forming a new question. *Why did you bother to warn us? Why were you so persistent all these years, if you think of us as aliens?*

Prince Kal flexed his fingers, staring at the swirls on the back of his hands.

It was more of an escape, at first. After the servants started serving us those Diurnals on a platter, my mother and I didn't want anything to do with our fortress anymore. We flew—just her and I —away from it all, to the other side of the sea. We should *have brought some others with us. Aro knows there were hundreds of enslaved Leather Skins and subjugated Nocturnals who would have loved to escape his regime too.*

This didn't make sense, though. Why the hell was there a whole *village* of Nocturnals if Prince Kal and his mother had flown off alone? For a moment, incest crossed Joah's mind, but no... not enough time had passed for the two to have reproduced so quickly. And two couldn't create *hundreds.*

"What's incest?" Damien asked aloud. Hickory gawked at him.

"Never you mind that," Misla said, glaring at Joah. "Go on, Prince."

My mother and I Moved with the night. We always loitered just behind the brink of sunset, never too far behind your new shiny general and his new shiny power. But we visited other communities of Nocturnals along the way. Some were whole cities to the south. Others were tribes to the north. No matter whether they Stayed or Moved every few decades, we kept hearing the same story over and over: a Nocturnal king from across the sea had sent stars flying over their heads, dropping acid on their people and land.

Joah imagined poison raining from the clouds and gave a low whistle. *That* was one way to piss off the whole world. It was also a fine way to keep all your subordinates from running off to other cities or tribes. Like an abuser killing off his victim's resources to the outside world.

When we told them what King Isce had done to the Diurnals, they were furious, Prince Kal continued. *They thought your kind strange and foreign too, but that perspective didn't make them feel better about your slaughter. We collected the most passionate ones along the way. Activists, artists, allies of all sorts. They wanted to come with us, to help stop it from happening again.* His internal voice cracked. *They've been helping us call out to your people for sixty years.*

So it was more than just guilt, the reason Queen Usai had been so intent on warning them. It was outrage. It was a fight for justice. It was an aro-wide attempt to halt evil in its tracks.

A lump bobbed in Joah's throat as they turned away from the metal star and began walking the High Road. A thick layer of moss now caked the pavement, muffling their footsteps.

It's as if we're already in the tunnel, huh? Misla said, smiling a little.

We've always been in a tunnel, in a way, Joah said. *Always heading in one direction, just following the High Road endlessly, blindly believing in General Deck —*

Again, Deckler's betrayal washed over him. Misla pursed her lips and nodded. Joah glanced sideways at her. His breath stuck inside his throat.

Her braids were knotted and frazzled. The ghost of a bruise still yellowed her eye. Dirt highlighted the smallest wrinkles in her forehead, and veins were starting to pop like tattoos in her temples. But she was somehow beautiful in her exhaustion, in her endless determination to keep marching forward, and Joah couldn't hide his urge to hold her again like they'd held each other in the conical tower. To touch her, to kiss her...

I'm sorry, he said, embarrassed, before his thoughts could expose more of this strange internal heat. Beside him, Damien stifled a snigger, and he sent a wordless warning at the boy.

I didn't hear anything, Misla said, passing him a wink.

A bluish glow the size of a coin highlighted their exit ahead. Joah let himself fall into musing silence as they approached it. He hadn't yearned for a woman since Blair. The desire felt awkward, clumsy, like he'd swallowed a lit cigar that was puffing out tendrils of guilt inside his stomach. He could just imagine it: his last night with Blair. She was whispering about babies, her lips cold against his earlobe, and her hands were creeping beneath his shirt, hardening him... but suddenly Misla's warm body flumped onto the quilt between them, and it was *her* fingers stroking his skin, and Blair dissolved in a wisp of moon-colored smoke.

Be prepared for anything, Prince Kal said, cutting through his visions.

Joah held up his rod. Misla gripped the ax with whitened knuckles. Hickory grumbled something about his tied hands, but nobody paid him attention as they ducked beneath stray fibermud tails hanging from the ceiling and entered the night.

Darkness had suffocated almost everything. Only the crooked remains of cotton trees rose toward the sky, which blazed with stars. As they crept down the High Road and passed these stumps, however, Joah saw tiny orange buds blossoming from the naked branches.

This phase of night is like grief, Prince Kal said. *It's as if the world has to grieve the loss of its sun before it can grow again. But after a few dozen moon cycles, the leaves come back. New grass grows. Animals you wouldn't dream of creep from their hideaways.* Kal stroked his rod. *That's why we have to be on the lookout. The Calic is the only beast that dares attack us in high numbers, but other things can rise from the mud if we're alone.*

Damien, it seemed, couldn't control his excitement as the conical tower rose in the distance. The boy's breath fogged in front of him in quick bursts.

This was where I first heard you clearly, he told Kal. *You told me how to find the door.*

Yes, Prince Kal said. *I sensed the Calic prowling around the outskirts of our camp and wanted you to hide out somewhere safe until I could reach you. But that didn't go quite as planned, did it?* Here, Kal glanced at Joah and Misla. No, it hadn't gone to plan—because Joah and

Misla had found the boy and frightened him into running away that very moon cycle.

As the tower loomed closer, Joah saw flicks of Damien's memories: he watched the boy stumble toward it and run his fingers along the outside wall, until he found a small notch and pressed his hand against the metal plate below it. Instantly, the walls slid apart with a rickety screech, revealing a gap like a popped-out tooth that now, cycles later, stared them in the face.

My father didn't want the Leather Skins getting in or out on their own, Prince Kal said, *so he made the door respond to cold fingerprints, not hot ones. In fact, the Leather Skins he sent to mine this sunsap never came back. He didn't want them spilling the secret of where the reserve was, see. There aren't many reserves as big as the one you're going to.*

"You mean the Leather Skins are still in there?" Misla asked, hushed, staring upward at the coned roof as if she could see watchful windows. "They could be in there right now? We didn't see any—"

Oh, my father wouldn't have let the Leather Skins live. After his guards obtained enough sunsap, he killed the ones who'd mined it before flying the starships back to our fortress by the sea. Prince Kal shrugged off his bag and tossed it to Damien, who caught it with quick fingers. *Go on in and see for yourself. I'm sure their skeletons are still there.*

"Hang on."

This was Hickory. He was whipping his head back and forth between Misla and Prince Kal, as if he could tell they'd been whispering to each other but didn't quite know what they were saying. "All this talk about something being in there. I need my hands free. What's the point of me coming along if I can't even punch a beast in the mouth, huh?"

"No," Joah said automatically, his jaw twitching with the effort to stop himself from punching *Hickory* in the mouth. "No way we're untying you."

Apparently there was a way, though. With a swift look at Prince Kal, Misla strode forward and stuffed the rusted handle of the old lantern into his mouth. Hickory tried to jerk away, but Kal held him in place until he bit down, eyes narrowed.

"I'll untie you," Misla said. She would have sounded sweet if her eyes hadn't been reflecting the glint of the ax now grasped with two hands. "But if that light falls, I won't hesitate to bury this blade into your heart. A blow for a blow, okay?" And she pointed at her chest, where her burn scar marred the soft place beneath the collar of her shirt. Hickory's doing.

Gagged by his own handle, he couldn't do anything but nod.

Joah wasn't going to make the mistake of undermining one of Misla's decisions again, but he couldn't quite look at her as he nodded goodbye to Prince Kal. It was enough to make his stomach writhe, the stench of Hickory's sweat and shit. For his wife's killer to walk beside them, free-handed? After the scene he'd come upon in the woods? Nauseating.

You can do it, Prince Kal said. *Just be wary, and not just of him. Remember, the Eternal Night may be... protective of the only thing keeping it alive for the next thirty years.*

Joah drew a deep breath, gripped his rod, and pressed forward into the tower. Misla, Damien, and Hickory followed.

Inside, bone fragments haloed that conical hole leading downward like a toilet bowl, but this time Joah focused on the bones he couldn't identify. As his eyes adjusted to the denser darkness, he squinted at a round one near his feet.

"Was this here the last time we were in here?"

They gathered around the object, which flickered in the light of Hickory's lantern. It was like a disk of shiny gray cartilage, umbrella-shaped and sprouting a stem of bone like a mushroom. Damien squatted to inspect it more closely.

"That's not a bone," he said solemnly. "It's a shell. Or *part* of a shell."

Gazing around, Joah saw dozens more littered around the room. He must have been too sick or worried to have noticed them the first time he had been here, but Damien was right—the objects were shells, and they had been abandoned here as surely as the skeletons of other creatures had.

The remains of Leather Skin slaves.

"I wouldn't—" Joah began, but Hickory had already bent to scoop up the shell at their feet. He held it by the stem and hugged it to his chest so that it looked like a shield.

His light didn't fall.

"Okay," Joah said, nodding to the edge of the hole in the ground. A narrow staircase wound down its rim into even more darkness. "You can go first, then."

Hickory grunted agreement and shuffled his way to the staircase. Joah wrapped his cloak tighter around himself as he followed suit. The hole seemed to exhale frost, and when he took his first step down, he felt like a man sinking through a frozen lake.

They moved carefully, pressed against the side of the winding wall, which roughened into dark, wet rock halfway down. The light from Hickory's lantern bobbed in front of them. Joah hadn't realized how much he had been depending on Prince Kal's skin until they reached the bottom, where murky water pooled on the ground. Here, the lantern only illuminated a few meters in front of them. A narrow channel, like a rocky throat, seemed to lead endlessly onward. Wiry white roots waved from the cracks in the rocks like hair in wind.

"Well, Glade?" Joah said. "See any booby traps? Are the walls going to collapse on us, or can we keep going?" He half-wanted to be told to stop, to turn around, to ascend.

Hickory struggled to talk through his rusted handle.

"There nothin' here. Keep going."

They splashed their way forward. The lantern flickered. The roots sprouting from the walls became thicker and longer, and they seemed to be swaying, wiggling like worms. Twice, Joah did a double take, thinking he'd seen a snake shoot from the mud as if to strike them. But no, it was just one of those tapered roots, and the lunge must have been a trick of the eye.

Hickory kept his Leather Skin shield in front of him. The air thickened the further they trekked, until puffs of hot air beat their faces. Hickory raised his shield. It blocked the worst of the heat, but the groundwater still wavered with steam that pricked their ankles.

There's something in here with us, Damien thought. His dark hair shined and curled with sweat. *I can tell by the—*

They turned a corner. Misla's sudden scream was gagged as something—thick and long and flexible—shot from the mud to wrap around her throat.

In that fractured moment when the spin of the aro slowed and Misla lurched backward toward the mud of the tunnel wall, Joah understood perfectly. It wasn't snakes or spiders or scorpions that squirmed beneath the conical tower. It was only the roots of the Eternal Night.

And the Eternal Night would defend itself from thieves.

Joah rushed forward as more roots, some thick as tubers, others skinny as vines, wrapped themselves around Misla's body, pinning her to the mud. He yanked at the one choking her throat, but it only tightened, and Joah felt the sticky mucus coating its wood like a leech.

"Get off her!" he bellowed, wrenching and punching and kicking at the things that strangled her. The rosy flush in her cheeks was draining to her neck. The roots had pinned her arms above her head, and even the ax she had been holding disappeared in the squirming mess.

The light behind him dropped. A hand shoved him backward.

"Take *that*, you little fucker," Hickory snarled.

He pressed the shell of his Leather Skin shield against the root around her neck. It contracted like a branded worm, shrinking back into the mud.

Misla gasped. One by one, Hickory pressed his shield against the roots until they shriveled or wilted, releasing her from her rigid confinement. Joah could hear a sharp *tssss* as the shield made contact with each one. The shell was hot, had been absorbing the heat ahead of them like a beetle's back. That was probably why the Leather Skins had been able to mine the sunsap—not just because they could withstand the heat, but because their shelled armor grew as hot as the sunsap itself and allowed them to pass undetected.

Joah fished his rod from a steaming puddle. He didn't remember dropping it, but it wouldn't have been any use against the roots anyway... the dart could have missed and struck Misla instead. Now he pointed the rod at Hickory's back as Misla slumped to the ground and Damien scrambled forward to help her up.

Hickory withdrew, saw Joah pointing his rod, and gave a wheezing laugh.

"You're really gonna kill me for saving your new lover?"

"No," Joah said, "but I'm going to keep this right here until Misla picks up her ax."

Hickory's laugh was broken by a cough, a hack, and a flying wad of spit that landed near Joah's shoes. "I have a *shield*, Cadshaw. Better think twice before one of those darts bounces off and gets you in the eye. Or... no, don't think twice. Just do it. Let's see."

He tossed the Leather Skin shell from hand to hand as if preparing for a sports game, but Misla had already seized the ax. She stood there, panting and gripping the weapon with both hands. A red bruise noosed her neck. For a moment, she looked at the dead lantern lying half-submerged in a pool of water at her feet and seemed to consider following through with her promise to kill Hickory despite his reason for dropping it. Then her shoulders sagged.

"The sunsap's got to be close," she rasped. The tears in her eyes swam with light: an orange glow highlighted a widening in the tunnel ahead, where more tapered roots swayed from the ceiling like tentacles. "Hickory, you go first with your shield. I'll follow with—"

"Misla," Joah started. "Let me do it. I'll chop those things to pieces if I have to."

"No, I've got this. You just watch *him.*" She jerked her head at Hickory. "Make sure he doesn't try anything funny." She threw a ragged braid over her shoulder. "Come on."

Joah didn't dare argue, not with that same fierce determination clenching her jaw like when she'd decided to go after Damien. They pressed on. The air shimmered with heat waves. Hickory held his shield out, but the shell could only block so much. Joah watched the back of Misla's cloak bloom with sweat as she swung at stray roots, and he couldn't help but gape in awe until beads of his own sweat rolled into his mouth—she'd been burned more than the rest of them, but still she plunged onward, wearing her newest burn like a goddamned necklace.

Don't make me blush, Misla sent back to him. *My face is hot enough as it is.*

Before long, the roots thickened into a squirming nest, crisscrossing and twisting and braiding together like the fibermud walls. Misla grunted as her movements quickened: raising the blade—

thwack. Raising the blade—*thwack.* Whenever a stubborn one tried to twine itself around her arms or legs, Hickory pressed his shield against it and the thing would cringe away.

The tunnel curved again. Misla chopped through a final thicket. They rounded the corner.

"I'll be damned," Joah whispered, hushed.

They were on the edge of what looked like an underground river spreading from left to right, where the tunnel walls had split into a T. The liquid was thick, bubbly, and golden, radiating a furnace-fueled heat that reminded Joah of the fabled molten rock spewing from mountains in the north. More roots waved from the muddy ceiling, while others had sunk into the slow-moving stream to drink the sunlight they could no longer capture from their leaves.

Damien crouched and ran a finger through the sludge on the edge of the river. He winced as it no doubt blistered his skin.

"Strange," he said, staring at the surface of sunsap with eyes that reflected its fire. "I don't know of a single bug or slug that could survive this heat..."

"But?" Joah said, suddenly anxious at the awed gape of the boy's mouth.

"But we've been following a trail of mucus for the last few dozen meters or so. Whatever made it went straight into the river. And whatever it is, it's bigger than us."

Indeed, Joah could see the thin white film slathering the rocks and mud at their soggy feet now that Damien had pointed it out. He shivered for the first time since entering the tower.

"Okay, let's move fast, then." He dropped his bag and rummaged through the capsules within. A single liter would fuel a hundred kilometers, Queen Usai had told them, so they'd only have to fill five or six to fly themselves to the Green Sea, where the sun would still be winking on the horizon. "Damien, can you hand me the capsules while I fill them?"

They got to work. Joah positioned a capsule on the edge of the river until tails of sunsap rolled into its open ceramic mouth. When the container had filled to the brim, he screwed the lid back on and returned it to Damien, who passed him another empty one. Misla and Hickory stood guard on either side of them, poised to shield or hack if something were to lunge their way.

It happened three capsules down. The tip of Joah's thumb grazed a drip of sunsap. He cursed, popped his thumb in his mouth, and hissed when it burnt his tongue.

Misla jolted toward him, relaxing her hold on the ax, and Joah saw the quick, spinning arc of Hickory's Leather Skin shield: it flew through the air, plopped into the sunsap, sank into its depths, and disappeared. Hickory had chucked it aside to spring for Misla's ax.

For half a second, they wrestled with it. The blade swung dangerously close to Misla's nose. Hickory yanked. Misla released her hold, fell back, and howled as the roots behind her twined around her waist and began reeling her in again.

"*No,*" Joah said.

He made to stand, dizzy with panic—how foolish could Hickory have been, tossing aside the Leather Skin shell that had saved Misla last time? But when Hickory staggered around with the ax raised like a flag, a crazed smile ripped his face, and Joah knew the man neither knew nor cared that the woman he used to love was clawing and retching and dying once again.

In a flash, Joah scooped up his rod, pointed it at Hickory's throat, and twisted. A dart whizzed outward but stuck into a swaying root above his head instead.

Hickory charged, swinging his old weapon with a roar. Joah raised one of his capsules like a shield, but it was no Leather Skin shell. The ceramic shattered as the blade struck it. The sunsap from within poured onto his chest, and he fell in a writhing spasm to the riverbank. Heat waves curled around his neck, and his chest pulsed with scorching agony.

"*I'll bury one of those sleek darts in your head,*" Hickory jeered. "Remember telling me that, Cadshaw? Remember *threatening* me?" He pressed his boot against Joah's throat, pinning him to the hot, rocky ground, searing his skull. "Don't make promises you can't keep, bitch."

Hickory brought up the ax again, and Joah's vision turned white. He knew he was about to die, knew his neck would split like his wife's had. From what seemed like far away, Misla was still shrieking.

Then the river exploded in a flurry of tiny, burning droplets that peppered Joah's cheeks with new pokers of pain.

Hickory howled. Joah squinted in disbelief at what he was seeing: a hunched figure rising from the depths of the sunsap, one hand clawing its way toward the bank with long, blackened fingers, the other pushing against the sunsap with the Leather Skin shield that Hickory had thrown in. The figure hoisted itself upward, sunsap dripping off its shelled body, and fixed its beetle-like eyes upon the ax reflecting fire in Hickory's hands. It didn't have a dozen eyes, but the rounded marks on its shell of a face *looked* like a dozen eyes.

Leather Skin, Damien cried from across the cavern.

Joah knew the boy was right, but he couldn't see how it was possible. *My father wouldn't have let the Leather Skins live,* Prince Kal had told them.

Yet here one stood, apparently immune to the heat of the sunsap, its hands curved like pincers, mucus oozing from its face. It wasn't leathery by any means, but its skin was like a snail's armor, like the shell in its grip.

"You." Hickory's hand trembled with the effort to point a finger at the creature.

You, the Leather Skin said back, a single voiceless word that escaped its mind like steam through volcanic cracks in the aro. It raised the shield in its pincer. *Where did you get this?*

Hickory, of course, didn't hear. "You," he said again, staggering around. Ruddy blotches had sprouted all over his face. "*You're* a Nocturnal. A true one—"

Stop. The Leather Skin pointed at Hickory's ax with a hairy finger. *Drop the weapon. There shall be no more murders here. This place is sacred.*

Joah tried to stand, but collapsed in a panting heap. He had to get to Misla. Across the cavern, Damien was pouring sunsap from the capsules onto the roots that bound her, but he was only succeeding in pissing the things off, it seemed; they would retract and snarl forward again, wrapping around Misla's ankles and wrists as she thrashed in their grip.

Joah began crawling toward them, never mind the mud that blistered his palms and knees through his pants. But Hickory saw him and seemed to decide, with a vicious scowl, to finish Joah off before attending to the monstrous creature before them. He raised his ax again.

The Leather Skin hurled his shield. It struck Hickory's raised wrists, and the ax spun from his hands, landing with a *thwump* a breath from Joah's fingers.

Hickory screamed and dove toward the Leather Skin instead, closing his hands around its shelled throat. The creature's eyes popped in their sockets for a moment, bloodied with shock—then it twisted, and soon both monsters were writhing in each other's grips.

Joah wrenched his gaze away from the humanoid insect that had once stared at him from the poster on General

Deckler's office wall. He crawled around the ax, grabbed the shield wobbling beside it, and dragged the thing toward Misla across the cavern. He shouldered Damien aside and pressed the shield against the roots coiled around her.

They retracted like worms touched by sunlight. Misla fell forward, coughing and gasping, onto her hands and knees.

"We need to fill the capsules," she panted, her voice hoarse, "and get the fuck out of here. This place is going to kill us." She made to stand, but crouched back down when the spinning mass of Hickory and the Leather Skin shot past them.

"You killed my grandfather," Hickory was panting. "They drew pictures of you." He rammed his fist into the other's ash-black jawline. "You're the Nocturnal I've been waiting for."

I'm not a Nocturnal, the Leather Skin spat, trying to close his pincers around Hickory's throat. *The Nocturnals killed everyone here but me.*

And Joah got flashes of the Leather Skin's memories: when King Isce's men had executed the others, this one had slipped away, had taken refuge in the sunsap and remained here for more than sixty years. But now the skeleton of one of its fellow slaves had sunk into its home, and the flicker of Hickory's blade had brought that violence back with blunt force.

So they spun in circles, a boulder-like man dancing with a humanoid creature on crooked scuttling spider legs. Hickory's fury had cracked his face into a million pieces, and the heat rash scaling his skin made him look less than human. He pummeled the other again and again, rooted in his belief that the creature in his grip was a Nocturnal, that it had killed his grandfather so long ago and sent Hickory's family cascading into poverty. Executing the Infected had never been enough for his revenge. Now he had the opportunity to kill the actual thing he thought he hated.

"Hickory," Joah choked out. "Hickory, open your mind."

Hickory didn't hear. He had knocked the Leather Skin to the ground and was thumping a fist into his face... a fist that bounced back; unfazed, the Leather Skin closed his pincers around Hickory's throat again and threw him sideways... They rolled closer to the sunsap.

"Hickory!" Joah was suddenly shouting. "*Listen* to him. He didn't kill your grandfather, it wasn't him! And the ones like him never wanted to! It's a whole lot more complicated, dammit! OPEN YOUR MIND AND LISTEN."

But Hickory either couldn't or wouldn't listen. He ripped himself from the Leather Skin's hold and plunged for his ax.

The Leather Skin barreled toward him and wrapped his arms around the man who would, if left unchecked, turn him into a headless corpse, as his fellows had been so long ago. The pair seemed to hover sideways in an embrace for a small eternity, the ax handle slipping from Glade's beefy fingers like a stubborn fish: going...going...gone.

Then Hickory and the Leather Skin toppled into the river as a single unit. The sunsap embraced them both in a slurping kiss, swallowing Hickory's scream whole.

Silence. Damien's eyes were round as moons. Misla was still panting. Holes riddled her clothes where the splatters of sunsap had burned her, adding to her collection of scars. Various parts of Joah's body flared with blistering heat. The chill of the Eternal Night sounded like bliss, yet he and the other two waited, breathless, for Hickory to emerge.

After a dozen heartbeats of silence, Joah knew he never would. The Leather Skin would be laying his body to rest beneath the blood of the Eternal Night.

He glanced at the remaining ceramic containers lying in the water at their feet.

They needed to fill the things and get away from this underground gut of fire before it cooked them. They needed to ride the starship to daybreak and save the Sunsetters from being killed or collected like cattle. But Joah felt mesmerized by Hickory's death. At how it had happened.

If Hickory had let himself become Infected, he would have known the truth of things. He wouldn't have gone for a guiltless Leather Skin. He wouldn't have raised the ax on Joah. Hell, he wouldn't have swung down on Blair's neck all those years ago. He would have heard her thoughts as Joah had led her—God, *led* her—to her death. He would have understood that the real threat was a corrupt general and a king waiting for them on the edge of the Green Sea, not a crazed woman in shackles or a slave who had been hiding from violence for over sixty years.

But Hickory had not opened his mind. And now he was gone. Blair's killer was gone. Misla's abuser was gone. The man who would have executed Damien with a smirk on his face was gone. He was gone along with the ignorance Joah might still be harboring if he'd never ventured into the Eternal Night.

All that remained now were the capsules of sunsap, the three of them holding each other, and a suffocating tunnel of boiling grief. And Joah was ready to find his way out of it.

"C'mon," he told the others. "We have a sunset to catch."

Sunrise

Someone was knocking on Aoif Deckler's door.

He ignored the noise, staring out his window at the mountainous shadows darkening the valley where he had forced his people to settle. He could smell the salt from here. Just beyond those cliffs, the sun was balancing on the edge of a great sea, a sea he had been yearning to taste again ever since his boots had crunched back on brittle sand fifty-eight years ago.

"General Deckler, sir," a voice called from behind the door. "Please."

He tried to ignore the wretched knocking, but his captain's voice whined through the wood incessantly. After a few more ticks from his wristwatch, Deckler withdrew his feet from his polished desk and slammed them to the frayed, thin carpet.

"Okay, fine, don't piss off," he boomed. "Why don't you come in, then, Lincoln? We can have ourselves a little tea party while we're at it. Act like princesses."

The door burst open. Captain Lincoln stood panting in his doorway, the hallway behind him strangely distorted—its walls had been dented during their most recent Move. A silver badge gleamed on his chest, his hair shined with gel, and his hands were naked of calluses.

"It's a woman from the Dirt Slums, General," Lincoln breathed. "She's going mad down in the office. Tearing her hair out, practically. Won't stop screaming that she wants to see you, and well..." Captain Lincoln massaged his lotioned hands together. "You sent most of our security ahead with the first wave. We don't have any jailhouses. Or handcuffs."

No, Deckler had not wanted the officers and retrievers to come running when the Nocturnals—or rather, the Nocturnal *slaves*—invaded the Dirt Slums. He had sent those individuals ahead to camp out with the scavengers and sailors on the edge of the Green Sea, where they'd be safe.

Captain Lincoln, on the other hand, would probably get snatched up in his haste to help the chosen victims. So would the Dirt Slummer apparently banging around his office downstairs.

"What's her name?" Deckler asked the captain, his eyes flicking open.

"Lupita Fertheli, General."

The name stirred something vaguely familiar in Deckler's chest. Ah, he needed a cigar. His fingers twitched toward his cabinet, where his last roll of tobacco lay tucked away—but no. When they sailed the sea and left this piece of the aro behind, he'd only get one smoke. Better to save it for something more disturbing, more frightening, than a piss-poor bitch of the slums.

Deckler grinned, opened his desk drawer, and popped a candy into his mouth. He rolled the thing from cheek to cheek until he felt his teeth turn blue.

"Send her up, Lincoln. Let's see what she has to say."

The captain bowed and scurried away, his footsteps clunking down the portable stairs past the bend in the hallway. Moments later, a door from below banged open. Lupita Fertheli's shrieks crashed into Deckler's office moments before the woman herself did.

"I can walk by *myself*, thank you very much."

Lupita yanked her elbow from Captain Lincoln's grasp, took one look at Deckler lounging in his office chair, and slammed the door behind her with a violent kick of her fraying sandal.

"Well, good evening," Deckler said, half-amused, half-irritated. "Or should I say good night?" He glanced out the window, where the cliffs cast pools of darkness. He imagined he could see the outlines of the ships Captain Lincoln's men had built on the shoreline.

"It *isn't* a good night," snarled Lupita Fertheli. Her hair stuck wildly in every direction, witch-like. The palms she slapped on Deckler's desk left grimy handprints on a stack of papers. Hatred and fury bandaged the grief lining her face. "My son is still missing."

"Is he, now?"

The gears clicked into place. *Yes.* This was the woman whose son Joah Cadshaw had been trying to find for the law enforcement office. Deckler himself had halted the investigation so he could send Cadshaw to do more important things, like getting the hell out of his way.

Judging by the repugnance pinching Lupita Fertheli's face, she already knew this.

"Where's Detective Cadshaw, General?" she asked now. Deckler felt a thrill of relief at the wobble infecting her voice. It wouldn't take long for the tears to flow, and when they did, she'd no longer seem to tower over him like a wiry-haired fortress.

"Cadshaw?" he asked, blinking up at her politely.

"Yes, *Cadshaw*. The one looking for my son. The one you sent away. I *know* he went to you after the Moving bells rang early. I *know* he left the community with another retriever. But I'm begging you— *begging* you..." And there it was: a glistening eye. "Tell me where Cadshaw is now," she said. "Has he found my Damien? Did h-he ever come b-back?"

"Listen, Lupita. It's Lupita, isn't it?" Deckler didn't wait for her to nod; he put a hand on the same wrinkled elbow she had yanked from Captain Lincoln. "I sent Joah out west to see if your son had... strayed. To see if he'd gone after the Nocturnals."

This was a lie, but when Lupita's shoulders sagged from their previous rigidity, he didn't regret it. He massaged her elbow, and she let him, sniffing up tears that wobbled on the edge of her nose. Such an *easy* lie. The truth hit harder, especially since he'd actually liked Cadshaw.

"But he didn't come back when I told him to, Lupita. Last I heard, he and Retriever Crane warned the grahsm miners about the early bells and continued west. The oil scavengers said they never saw them. As far as I know, Cadshaw's still searching for your son."

Or being hacked to pieces, he didn't add when Lupita split into sobs. He had his own suspicions about the fate of Joah Cadshaw: the man's enemy, the one who'd cut off his wife's head, hadn't returned from his western duties either. Just *poof.* Gone. Deckler had chuckled a little to think that the two would meet again when he'd sent Joah that direction, but now that neither had returned, it wasn't hard to imagine a bloody battle in the woods at sunset.

Ah, well. There were more important things. Like ships. Or the invasion that would tear through the valley within the next arcsec. Or the sobbing wench before him.

"Listen, Lupita, if you have an arcsec to spare, I could have my secretary make you some tea. Our herbalists found a new kind of mint on the way here, I'm sure it would help calm you."

He didn't know what made him say it. Why should he care for a grubby life like hers? The sooner she left his office, the sooner he could focus on his impending date with the Nocturnal king. But something in her wild, crazed face mirrored the smut of that horrible season after his mother's death and before he became general. When he had been poor and hungry and scared too.

Lupita Fertheli wrenched her elbow away from his stroking thumb, her eyebrows hardening. For a mad moment, she looked the same shade of sick Deckler's own mother had been so long ago. Flames pierced her eyes, and she thrust her chin in the air.

"I won't stay here if you don't have answers. I'm missing my *son*, dammit, and if you don't know what happened to Detective Cadshaw, I'll find someone who does."

She whipped around. Deckler's eyes followed her trembling figure to the door.

"Suit yourself," he said somberly, after one of those sandals had kicked it shut again.

He waited for the night to begin with tightly pressed fingertips. Nobody disturbed him again. He opened his drawer, popped more candy in his mouth, rolled it along his gums. The clock ticked. The shadows deepened. Eventually, Deckler hoisted himself up and approached the cabinet. He glanced at the glossy poster hanging above it, that many-eyed figure leering at him behind lamination. The image cheered him up. It was funny, really... he'd spent the last sixty years teaching his students at the Retrieving Institute that the creature painted on the poster was a Nocturnal: as far from the truth as day was to night.

With a whistle, he opened the cabinet door.

When the clock struck three degrees, smoke was already curling toward Deckler's ceiling. It was not quite nighttime, but the cliffs blocking the sun bathed them in a rich darkness. He strode to his window and thrust it open, inhaling that smell of salt and ocean breeze.

From the crevices in the distant cliffs, disfigured shadows scuttled into the valley. They wended their way between wheeled structures, into the slums that had Moved from *there* to *here*.

When the first screams rent the air, Deckler looked back at his pinned poster and winked at it, as if enjoying a silent joke with an old friend.

Joah watched the ground shrink through frosted windows.

As they rose above the netted treetops, the landscape became a mass of intersecting light. Patches of foliage were re-growing where their sun counterparts had died. Blades and leaves and trees glowed with the energy their roots had sucked from the ground. The plants were feeding off the reservoir of sunsap they had collected during the thirty-year day.

That same sunsap now fueled Joah's flight through the clouds.

As the clouds thickened, mist swathed his view of the aro below. He withdrew from the window and turned to find Prince Kal explaining various parts of the starship to a wide-eyed Damien Fertheli: there was the control system, slathered in buttons and knobs more complex than any vehicle Joah had ever seen; and over *there* were the storage bins, metal compartments filled with canned sugar water, spare spider silk cloaks, and weapons.

I can take you up to see the generator, if you'd like, Kal told the boy.

Even after spending a whole season with the Nocturnals, Joah still marveled at the words hissing, not from the prince's lips, but from his mind. Telepathy suited the circumstance, though. It was hard to hear voices over the rattling of the starship as they flew.

Oh, yes, please, Damien said, obviously trying not to appear too eager. His face remained nonchalant, but his thoughts quivered with excitement. *I mean, why not?*

This way, then.

Prince Kal pulled a lever dangling from the ceiling. A narrow ladder unfolded itself from the upper floor, and Kal mounted it, motioning for Damien to follow.

When he and the boy had disappeared into the crawlspace above, Joah turned to Misla, who was fingering the rough wooden edges of the table quivering in the middle of the room.

"Are you alright?" he asked, touching the other end of the table. His mind mimicked his tongue, so he knew she'd be able to hear him as clearly is if he were whispering into her ear.

She had bathed since they had retrieved the sunsap from underground. Her hair fell in tight waves below her breasts, and she wore a honied blue dress made from one of the queen Nocturnal's old cloaks. A bruise spiraled around her neck where the creatural roots had strangled her below the aro. Beneath her dress, she wore another scar, the remnants of an abuser now gone.

Joah moved closer. She gave a hesitant smile.

"I feel sick, to be honest."

"Couldn't have anything to do with the fact that we're zooming through the air faster than the sun moves across the sky, could it?" Joah asked.

Her lips twitched.

"Could be. Or maybe it's because I'm about to confront the general I swore an oath to and tell him his ass is fried if he doesn't step down. *That* would make anyone want to puke."

"Hey, you know that's not part of the plan."

No, Deckler would never step down. They all knew that, even Damien. Their plan was no longer to fly to the Sunsetters and dissuade their general from a deed he'd been planning for six decades. They were heading southeast, yes, but toward King Isce's fortress instead, where they would kill the Nocturnal king before he could give his orders. If they made it in time, that was. And if they *could* kill him.

"Don't," said Misla, clasping her stomach. "I really *might* puke."

Again, Joah felt that desire to hold her, or be held by her, or do more than stare at her with a table between them. But he swallowed his thoughts and said, "Why don't you go to bed, then? If Prince

Kal is right about how fast this thing flies, we'll be there in a dozen arcsecs."

"Yeah, okay."

Swaying a little, she crossed the circular room and approached one of the rounded outlines by the control panel. She pressed her cold palm against it. The wall slid upward obediently, revealing one of the tiny sleeping compartments Prince Kal had shown them earlier.

She paused outside the door, jolting as the starship rocked violently.

Will you come with me, Detective Cadshaw?

Joah's heart raged inside him, louder and more fearsome than Moving bells could ever be. He clutched the table's edge, more to steady his mind than his body. Outside, rain began to thrash against the glass, and the mist flared with occasional bursts of light.

I mean, why not? he said in the same offhand tone that Damien had expressed.

She rolled her eyes and ducked her way into the compartment, which housed a pull-down cot beneath some overhanging shelves. She crawled onto the mattress, sinking into its spongy material. Joah followed. He could hear the faint drone of Prince Kal and Damien's thoughts in the crawlspace above, but when he lowered the compartment door behind him, the buzz of their conversation faded. The only sound in here, it seemed, was Misla breathing.

He sank onto the bed, reaching out to find her in the denseness of this new, rich darkness. His hand found her shoulder; his fingers traced her neck, hovered over the bruise, and worked their way up to her chin, her lips. Hot desire shuddered through him, as if he'd inhaled sunsap.

She grabbed the back of his neck and pulled him onto her, and then their lips brushed against each other, and her thighs were wrapping around his waist, drawing him closer.

I want you, they said together. Their thoughts were merging, twisting and twining like the glowing designs of the aro during the Eternal Night. And they were kissing—he was tasting her, and she smelled like sweetened sunshine. *Misla, Misla, Misla.* He pulled up her dress, and...

In the darkness, it might have been Blair, the corpse of his dead wife lying in his bed, running fingers through his hair, muttering that she wanted a baby...

And Misla's thoughts scampered with panic too. In the darkness, it might have been Hickory, the corpse of her ex-lover bowing over her with that greedy stench of rape wafting from his tongue, ready to sink rotting teeth into the burn scar he had inflicted upon her...

They broke apart, gasping for breath.

No! Joah cried.

No, no, no, Misla moaned.

Tears scorched Joah's cheeks as he rolled away. He had thought he was over his wife, that he'd come to accept her death. And God, he really *did* love Misla. But his body shook with tremors from that morbid vision, and he knew he had *not* healed, had not yet reached the light at the end of his vast and monstrous tunnel.

Neither have I, Misla said. She was crying too, her breath hiccupping as their mingled tears dampened the pillows. She still felt haunted by her own personal chasm of darkness too.

"What do we do?" Joah whispered out loud.

They found each other's hands as the walls gave a nasty jolt.

"We help each other find the light," Misla said.

He nodded, turned toward her, wrapped his arms around her waist and buried his face in her neck. Yes, they would help each other find the light. He closed his eyes.

They'd walk the tunnel together, even if it felt like that walk would never end.

When they finally shot from the clouds, sunset pierced them through the windows.

Joah, Misla, and Damien squinted, shielding their eyes with their hands. Prince Kal donned his hood and clipped the edges of his cloak together, skulking in the shadows.

I can't touch the control panel anymore, the Nocturnal said, nodding at the stream of thin, orange light running from the windowpane to the many knobs and buttons. *One of you will need to follow my instructions to land. We're almost there.*

"I'll do it," Damien said.

Joah and Misla glanced at each other, but the boy had pinched his eyebrows together in obvious determination. With a unified nod, they stationed themselves on either side of him, ready to pounce on the panel if he ever became overwhelmed.

Okay, see that gear shift in the upper left corner? Yes, that's the one. Put it in low.

Damien did as Prince Kal commanded, his forehead wrinkled with concentration. He pulled levers, pressed knobs, and tapped keys with nimble hands. Soon they were plunging into a maze of cliffs and valleys and winding rivulets.

"Look," Misla said with a half-laugh, pointing, "I think it's that river we were going to float. The one that ran by the grahsm cavern. See how it's heading southeast."

Sure enough, a widespread snake of water glittered between canyons, and it led to—

"Oh," Joah breathed.

The horizon expanded as they descended, winking with pink light. And the sun—that brilliant bowl of orange Joah had so missed—teetered on the edge of a sea he had only ever heard stories about. It was, he thought as he stared out the window, like an upside-down sky, filled with rippled green water and sprinkled with stars. The fabled Green Sea.

Hard left, Prince Kal said. *We don't want to land on my father's front lawn.*

Damien drove the starship into a gulch surrounded by walls of rock. With Prince Kal's thoughts puppeteering his bony arms, the boy landed the contraption beside a twisting stream, where bushes and scrubs throttled its pebbled bank.

Now go, Prince Kal said, sinking into a crouch against the wall. *I can't go too near the castle, or my father might sense me. This stream leads straight to his fortress. And remember…* They turned to look at him as they gathered their packs and rods. His eyes were mere violet slits within the darkness of his hood. *You may find it difficult to remember both languages without a Nocturnal by your side. Don't let yourself get disoriented. Find your tongue.*

A cold chill spread through Joah's abdomen at this newest thought. Of course. He had become so accustomed to using telepathy and his tongue, both with ease, that he had forgotten how Damien had described the Nocturnal language away from the Nocturnals: *"It's like somebody's calling your name through the far end of a tunnel."*

"Hopefully we'll find King Isce right away, then," Joah said grimly.

The star's double doors slid upward, steaming. Joah, Misla, and Damien clambered onto the rocks below, leaving the prince behind. The stream gurgled to their right, but they couldn't see past the tangled shrubbery congesting its bank.

"We'll follow the sound," Misla said, hitching her pack higher up her back. Joah adjusted his too and nodded. Inside their many hand-stitched pockets were packets of seeds, water cans, ropes of fibermud, and cloaks. But they clutched the most important tagalongs in their hands as they started down the narrow channel of pebbles between shrubbery and cliff: rods with darts coated in sunsap that they would shoot at King Isce when they encountered him.

The gulley twisted this way and that, narrowing and widening, sometimes speared with orange light, other times bathed in twilight shadows. As they trudged forward, the greenery thickened, and mud squelched beneath their shoes. They began ducking beneath gnarled branches, pushing through the thorny arms of bushes, clambering over moss-cloaked boulders in their path.

The foliage clotted like a shield. Spikes poked from stems, some the size of Joah's thumb, others needle-like and hairy, reminding him all too well of the Leather Skin living within the depths of the sunsap. Hickory's ax would have suited them well now, but they had left it lying in the water in the underground tunnel along with the broken shards of ceramic.

"C'mon, let's take the stream," Misla muttered.

They pushed their way to the bank and splashed into piercingly cold, glass-clear water, which rose up to Joah's knees. After a few arcsecs of following the current, their hands rigid around their rods, Damien whispered, "What's that smell?"

The stream had spread out like melting butter. The air tasted like salt and moss and something undeniably slimy. But it was fresh too, and Joah inhaled deeply.

"I think it's the Green Sea. We should be—"

They rounded a corner and stumbled to a stop, squinting at the sudden slap of naked sunset. The gulley had opened to a coastline spreading eternally in either direction. The stream itself joined an immense, lazy body of water up ahead, which met the sea with the tenderness of a long-lost lover's kiss. Soaring birds dotted the sky above the harbor.

And to their left, a vast, interconnected collection of turrets and towers lined the coast. This was King Isce's fortress, where the Nocturnal, his subjects, and his slaves Stayed.

"Okay, Kal said the cellar looks like a half-moon," Misla said, pointing.

One of the towers up ahead, separated from the rest, curved like a stone horseshoe. This was how Prince Kal had told them to enter the fortress. The cellar would lead to the kitchens, which would help them bypass any guards that might be standing by the front doors.

Joah nodded. They stooped low and trudged through the stream until it meandered right. Then they clambered onto the muddy grass and dashed toward that half-moon tower.

Joah's ears pounded with the impending crash of the sea. He didn't want to face King Isce. More than that, though, he didn't want to witness what lay inside that cellar. They had *planned* to gather any remaining human bones to bring back to the community. Proof of Deckler's treachery. Of their looming doom. But as they neared the cellar, Joah's heart sunk with a tingling suspicion that perhaps they were too late. Perhaps the invasion had already begun.

Okay, who wants to do the honors? he asked, his tongue too dry to speak aloud.

They had scurried into the cellar's shadows. Vines crawled up the stone, smothering the outline of those circular doors lining the curve of walls. One door stood naked, though, the vines around it snapped in pieces, as if someone—or something—had already pushed its brute way inside. Joah's head buzzed. He tried to expel his thoughts, but they resounded differently inside his ears. Weaker.

I'll do it, Damien said.

The boy was about to push his cold palm against the door when movement on either side of them made him flinch back. Two shapes emerged from the deepest thickness of vines: shelled bodies, hairy legs, imprints on their faces like many-eyed insects.

The Leather Skins stared at them. They didn't say anything, but Joah could hear the faint drone of their thoughts anyhow, like frantic voices behind closed doors.

The deed was done. It was too late. They, the Leather Skins, had been forced into the invasion, had hauled masses of bodies to this cellar. Their buggy eyes seemed to be bleeding a sour green pus, as if they had been hurt in the process.

Joah's head buzzed and buzzed, but he managed to say, *Get out of here, all of you. We're going to get rid of him. Head north. You'll find some ships. Steal one. Sail your way back to daytime.* He swallowed thickly, choking on tears. They could afford for the Leather Skins to steal a ship because the Dirt Slummers had already been taken. *We won't be far behind.*

For a moment, he thought they were going to close their pincers around his throat. But with a ticking, clicking sound, they withdrew hesitantly, then scuttled lopsidedly away.

Damien slapped the door in his haste to get inside, where his mother's body would no doubt be lying among bones. The door obeyed, grinding upward until a mouth-shaped hole opened in the stone before them.

Joah had a split second to process the heated, stifled darkness inside. Bodies stirred within the cellar's black abyss. There came the sound of grinding bones, clattering rocks, and clinking chains. Damien sucked in a breath, and Misla reached out an uncertain palm...

Then someone screamed.

Before Joah could back away, a hand emerged from the darkness within and jerked him inside. He hollered, twisting blindly. He felt his rod wrenched from his grip. Misla and Damien shouted beside him. The door behind them lowered with a resolute *thunk*.

"What are you *doing*? You can't let them see us," growled a horribly familiar voice. It was gravelly and gruff, and it belonged to the person now clutching Joah's shoulder, forcing him deeper into the belly of the cellar. "To the honest depths of hell, I can't believe it. Detective Cadshaw and Retriever Crane. I thought you two were dead. And this little boy must be—"

"Damien!" a woman shrieked.

The buzzing in Joah's head swelled. He clamped hands over his ears, and realized, too late, that his pack was gone. He felt, rather than saw, a woman tear from the mass of huddled bodies surrounding them. He heard Damien cry out and cling to his mother, reunited at last.

But his mind couldn't comprehend what was happening, and Misla's own confusion met his like a tentacle of thought groping for land, for something to cling to in this darkness.

Why was General Aoif Deckler in the cellar with the very people he had handed over?

Why were the people—the living, breathing people—here at all? Joah had been prepared for the stink of rotting bodies, not for the stench of sweat and piss.

What are you doing, Deckler? he tried to rasp, but he couldn't find his tongue.

His foot lurched forward, kicking something small and hard on the floor. At the same time, the people around him began murmuring, and Deckler boomed, "I appreciate you trying to save us, retrievers, but we have a plan. You could have been *seen*, sneaking in like that."

What are you talking about? Joah tried to ask, but once again, his lips couldn't move.

Deckler seemed to hear him, though, and it was this, more than anything else, that spread ribbons of fear throughout Joah's body. He was immobilized, caught between two languages, but *Deckler* knew how to execute both perfectly. *Deckler* was still playing his game.

"If they see us trying to escape, we have no chance," the general said, his voice carrying throughout the cellar. Lupita muffled her sobs against Damien's hair. "But when they come in *here* to butcher us, they'll be caught unawares. They don't know we've escaped our chains, see. They won't know what's coming. It's our only chance at getting the hell out of here."

So that was it. Joah wobbled on his feet, dizzy from the buzzing in his ears. Aoif Deckler was still playing hero. The disappearance of half his community would have looked suspicious to the rest— had perhaps been too suspicious *last* time —so he had developed a new plan with King Isce. One that involved his own acting skills. He had been kidnapped with the rest of his people, dragged to this cellar, and locked inside. He had freed his own prisoners from their chains and helped them develop a plan of escape.

But Deckler wasn't planning on winning. *He* would survive, along with a few witnesses, who would report back to the rest of the community that their dear, valiant general had done everything he could to rescue them from the nighttime monsters.

Joah wanted to scream. To curse. To charge at his ex-boss.

He couldn't move. Misla was a statue beside him, and Damien had frozen in his mother's arms. General Deckler's voice hissed inside his head, stabbing him with needles of pain.

It's no good, Joah. Your little plan. Forget it, and you can be one of the few that live.

Joah closed his eyes, though it made no difference in the darkness. He remembered Prince Kal's words: *Don't let yourself get disoriented. Find your tongue.*

Yes, if he were to save these people from pointless butchering—if he were to convince them that Deckler was lying, that their best chance at escape was to lift the door again and stream toward the cliffs— he'd have to find his tongue.

He opened and closed his mouth, ignoring the increased muttering of the crowded bodies. Shapes emerged beneath his closed lids: he was on the High Road, surrounded by swarms of eager onlookers, but he was not leading his wife to the executioner's block. He was leading *himself*, his own handcuffs cutting into his wrists, his footsteps slow, clunky, deliberate.

"Warn you," he choked out now, opening his eyes. "Got to."

The cellar hushed. Deckler withdrew his hand from Joah's shoulder.

"What is this?" the general whispered, a cruel coldness hidden beneath his façade of shock and suspicion. "You'd like to warn us? Of what?"

"Warn you," Joah spluttered again, lurching forward.

"Scary," Damien piped up from the crook of his mother's arms.

"D-don't listen," Misla said, breathing fast. "Don't listen. Don't listen. Don't listen."

And now the muttering in the cellar rose to match the pounding buzz in Joah's ears, and somebody cried out, "They sound Infected!" and Lupita gasped and wailed.

Find your tongue, find your tongue, find your tongue, Joah begged himself, but it was too dark to find his tongue, and the prisoners were reeling, shouting insults, throwing rocks at Joah's legs. Somewhere in the back, a child wailed, and a mother said *shhh*, but the insults rose to a roar.

"Grab them," Deckler commanded. "They *are* Infected."

Damien was wrenched from his mother. Joah's wrists were pinned behind his back. He was forced to his knees between the boy and Misla, where fragments of bones stabbed his ankles, as if shattered pieces of glass coated the cellar floor. Lupita screamed.

"They'll ruin our plans," Deckler said, his voice smooth with apathy.

The prisoners responded with screeches of desperation. Joah did not blame them. They had been kidnapped by strange, scuttling creatures and forced into a cellar like pigs to a slaughterhouse. In their eyes, the Infected were threats now more than ever.

"The Nocturnals will be here any minute," Deckler said. "These three will only help them kill us. We have to get rid of them before that happens."

"*No!*" Lupita wailed, plunging forward.

Deckler ignored her, raising something into the air. As Joah's eyes finally adjusted to this new darkness, he made out the outline of a handheld saw—

the same tool Deckler must have used to break the chains—bearing down upon Damien's neck.

Lupita threw herself over her son. The saw's serrated edge lodged in her neck.

"NO!" Damien roared. "MOM. NO."

Before Joah could jolt or even process what had happened, several circles of light shot into the cellar like a dozen violent stars. The outlines of a hundred Nocturnal bodies flowed into the cellar, the glowing designs on their skin glinting off the cleavers in their hands. They were cloak-less, and their figures blended together in a whirl of chaotic light.

The prisoners shrieked, bumping into each other, trying to escape like caged chickens. They had expected their kidnappers, the enslaved Leather Skins, not these new vulture-like creatures whose arms rose and fell like wings. Some tried to stab their butchers with tapered bones, but the maze of light was dizzying, and cleavers cracked into skulls with the increased rapidity of popping corn.

Joah looked up, bleary. He saw General Deckler standing in the middle of the cellar, his hacksaw dripping with Lupita's blood. He was standing shoulder-to-shoulder with a Nocturnal whose designs twisted and flared like a lair of glowing baby serpents.

King Isce grinned as he surveyed the massacre.

Find your tongue, find your tongue, find your tongue, Joah cried within himself. But it was no longer his tongue that he needed. He put his forehead to the cellar floor and let his thoughts explode, so that even some of the Nocturnals paused, their cleavers quivering in midair.

PRINCE KAL, WE NEED YOU.

His silent cry rippled through the stone of the cellar, soared against the current of the stream, weaved between foliage. It re-traveled the length of the gulley, found the starship, and embraced the cloaked figure hunkered within it.

King Isce looked up. His violet eyes narrowed when he met Joah's gaze. He had heard. He knew his long-lost heir was somewhere nearby, knew that Joah had just contacted him.

The Nocturnal king swept toward him. Joah could hear Misla gasping beside him, and Damien weeping into his mother's body, which still lay draped over the boy like a shield of flesh. He, Joah, wanted to remember his light when he finally met the dark tendrils of death.

He spread his freed hands to try to touch the woman and boy he'd come to love—

The walls shook, and *BOOM*. The world blasted apart.

A great star burst through the cellar's eastern walls, crumbling the stone and roof in a blaze of fire, exposing them to the spears of sunset's light. Prince Kal drove his ship into the ground, and it exploded on impact, sprays of sunsap flying like shards of sky.

Joah grabbed Misla and Damien, pulled them closer. Around them, King Isce's butchers clawed at blisters blossoming on their skin. King Isce himself had halted; his skin was blackening, falling to the floor in scabbed flakes as the sunset pierced him.

The king half-turned, seeming to realize, too late, what his son had done.

Kill him, he murmured.

Then his body crumbled. It collapsed into a heap of ash on the floor. And all around him, his soldiers crumbled too, until all that remained were piles of ashes, the mangled bodies of prisoners, and a handful of survivors wailing through the smoke and dust.

General Deckler himself swayed on the spot. Joah groped for his fallen rod, which lay in a heap of cinders, and aimed it at him. He was going to twist and shoot. He was going to kill the general he had obeyed and admired his whole life with a dart smothered in sunsap.

Before he could force his hands to move, Deckler's hacksaw dropped from his fingers. It landed on a pile of ashes with a soft thud. Blood spiraled around Deckler's neck. He staggered forward, then collapsed as suddenly and violently as the starship had.

Joah lowered his rod. He saw what stuck from the back of his skull, and understood.

King Isce's last command had been *kill him*. One of his butchers had stuck his cleaver into the head of the man who had failed his king. There had never been any true alliance, only a kind of hunger and greed that couldn't endure even the weakest streams of light.

"Are you okay? Are you hurt?"

Both Misla and Damien were sobbing into his chest. His own body shook as he rocked them. Deckler and Lupita were dead. King Isce had disintegrated. Prince Kal had been blasted apart. They had only managed to save a few dozen prisoners from the carnage. If they didn't get to the rest of the community soon and start sailing, that precious sun would leave them behind once again.

"It'll be okay," Joah said. "We'll find our way out of here. It'll be okay."

And he realized, despite the smoking destruction around him, that he had found his voice.

The water roared around them as the ships plunged eastward.

Joah stood beneath the foremast, watching those little white stars jump along the distant horizon. The sun had become a darkened sliver, preparing to leave them behind forever. But they hadn't let it completely shrivel into darkness. As they sailed onward, it thickened and rose until the Green Sea became a twinkling pool of orange and pink and purple.

He sensed the collective gasp of those on board, the halting of progress to watch the sun's ascent. Eventually, a woman joined him, curling her fingers around the railing beside him.

"Quite the sunset, isn't it?" Misla sighed.

Her hair hung in loose waves over her shoulders. The sunbeams made her skin appear golden, her cheeks like two glowing coins. Joah put his arm around her waist, pulled her closer, and pressed his lips against her temple. A long journey still stretched before them, but he felt peace—maybe even a little excitement—that they would cross this sea together.

"Yes, it's quite the sunset," he agreed.

"It's not a sunset anymore." Damien had appeared on Misla's other side, tiptoeing to see over the handrail. He wore a newly stitched green shirt, which had been emblazoned with the face of a reptilian cat: not just an homage to the Calic they had killed in the Eternal Night, but a reminder that darkness teemed with good *and* bad, hopeful civility *and* wild desperation. "It's technically a sun*rise*," he said. "That's what you call it when things get brighter."

"Aren't you supposed to be in school?" Joah growled.

There were a few classrooms on the lower deck for the children on board: windowless, of course, so that the students wouldn't become distracted by the sea.

"I gave Mrs. Zemukil the slip," Damien said matter-of-factly. He was barefoot, Joah noticed, his toes somehow streaked with dirt. As usual. "I wanted to see it. The dawn."

"And how'd you manage to give your teacher the slip?" Misla asked, folding her arms.

"Oh, I just passed Timby Jenkins a note. No big deal." When Misla cocked a threatening eyebrow, he added, "It was a dare, that's all. I bet him he couldn't burp a hundred times within the next arcsec. Well, Mrs. Zemukil had to stop writing on the board after his seventh burp. By his twentieth, she was yelling too hard to notice me sneak away."

Joah tried not to chuckle, but his mouth twitched.

"Watch out, Misla," he warned as the breeze picked up, smacking his face with salt. "This kid's going to be general one day. Mark my words."

They hadn't elected a new general yet. After Joah and Misla had explained to the remaining prisoners in the cellar about Deckler's arrangement with King Isce, they had agreed that escaping the fortress and boarding these ships were more pressing matters. But one of the survivors, a certain Captain Lincoln, had assumed temporary command, and *he* was the one who had convinced the rest of the Sunsetters of the truth, even with the community in disarray: between the attack on the Dirt Slums, the disappearance of their general, and a horde of Leather Skins swarming one of their three ships and taking off with it, they had been in an uproar.

But Captain Lincoln had calmed them. He had told them the truth in a giant assembly by the *shoosh* of waves, organized the remaining ships' takeoffs, and arranged for the planting of their Nocturnal seeds onboard. There weren't any penned animals aboard—no, that would've reminded them all too much of their own recent captivity—but a garden arena on the main deck sprouted with various squashes and herbs, reminding Joah of Prince Kal and the other Nocturnals who had chased them around the aro to warn them of the darkness ahead.

"I hope Queen Usai gets our message," Misla murmured, as if she could read his thoughts. Maybe a small part of her still could, although all three of them had lost their sense of the soundless Nocturnal language, like water leaking through outspread hands.

"She will," Joah assured her.

While Captain Lincoln had been busy organizing the ships, Joah and Misla had snuck into the main, unguarded fortress, where they'd found a young cloaked Nocturnal hovering near a window. With their last remaining telepathic breath, they had told her to wait for her new Majesty, a queen by the name of Usai, who would soon come along to resume King Isce's place.

The Nocturnal had taken flight, cloak flapping behind her as she raced down the hall and disappeared around a corner. But Joah had sensed the delight squirming beneath her terror, the understanding that King Isce was gone and the aliens would be leaving soon.

"I just hate to think of Queen Usai finding the remains of that Shooting Star," Misla said.

They all fell silent, immersing themselves in the crash of water and wind. Behind them, activities were resuming: gardeners returned to the arena, Captain Lincoln continued shouting orders, and helmsmen raced to and fro. The deck creaked with movement and life.

Joah didn't wrench his eyes from the horizon, though. The three of them deserved to see it expand, he thought, to feel the sunshine warm their faces. Their tragedies had snatched away that warmth for so long, after all. They deserved to feel daylight's ripe embrace.

So with Misla and Damien beside him, with the Eternal Night behind him, he watched the distant dawn yawn itself to life until the moon rose into its new bright sky.

About the author

About the author

Mariah Montoya is a writer and new mother from Idaho. She loves watching movies and losing at chess games on cold, blustery days. On sunny ones, you can find her running with her husband and a stroller along the Boise river. You can't convince her to use Twitter, but she's sometimes on Instagram @mariah_author.

About the story

I first thought of the idea of an "Eternal Night" and the creatures who might live in it during a hike through the woods with my mom and sisters. We had done that thing you should never do, where you look at the next hill or bend and go, "Let's just see what's on the other side of that___, and then we'll turn around," a bunch of times, until you've gone further than you should have. It was only when shadows started checkering the barely-existent trail that we finally did turn around. On the way back, I thought, what if we can't find camp before dark? And then: what if the dark lasts forever?

I overthink things, as you may have guessed. We made it back to our tents before sunset, and no one at the camp had even missed us.

Copyright

Title information

The Nocturnals

ISBN: 978-1-64076-072-1 (e-book)
ISBN: 978-1-64076-078-3 (paperback)
ISBN: 978-1-64076-079-0 (hardcover)

Copyright

Works of fiction

All rights reserved

The authors and artists worked hard to create this work for your enjoyment. Please respect their work and their rights by using only authorized copies. If you would like to share this material with others, please buy them a copy.

Moral rights asserted

Each author whose work is included in this book has asserted their moral rights, including the right to be identified as the author of their respective work(s).

Publisher

Vestige is an imprint of
Metaphorosis Publishing
Neskowin, OR, USA

www.metaphorosis.com

"Metaphorosis" is a registered trademark.

Discounts available

Substantial discounts are available for educational institutions, including writing workshops. Discounts are also available for quantity purchases. For details, contact Metaphorosis at metaphorosis.com/about

Metaphorosis Publishing

Metaphorosis offers beautifully written science fiction and fantasy. Our imprints include:

Metaphorosis Magazine

Plant Based Press

Verdage

Vestige

Help keep Metaphorosis running at Patreon.com/metaphorosis

See more about some of our books on the following pages.

Metaphorosis

a magazine of speculative fiction

Metaphorosis is an online speculative fiction magazine dedicated to quality writing. We publish an original story every week, along with author bios, interviews, and notes on story origins. Come and see us online at magazine.Metaphorosis.com

Keep Metaphorosis running! Support us at
Patreon.com/metaphorosis

You can also find us at:
Twitter: @MetaphorosisMag,
@MetaphorosisRev, @Metaphorosis
Facebook:
www.facebook.com/metaphorosis

Plant Based Press

Vegan-friendly science fiction and fantasy.

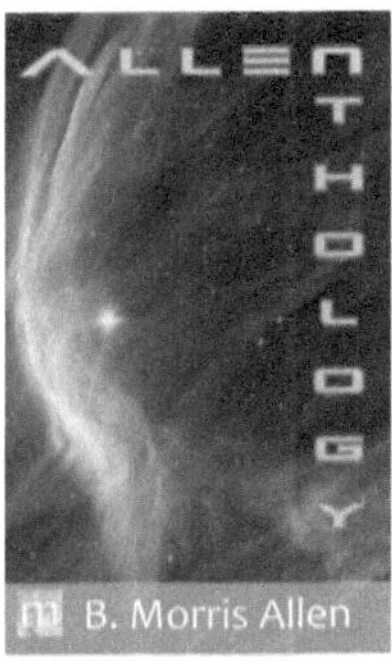

Susurrus

A darkly romantic story of magic, love, and suffering.

Allenthology: Volume I

A quarter century of SFF from B. Morris Allen

Best Vegan Science Fiction & Fantasy, 2016-2020

Verdage

Science fiction and fantasy books for writers – full of great stories, but with an additional focus on the craft of speculative fiction writing.

Reading 5X5 x2

Duets

How do authors' voices change when they collaborate?

Stories by Evan Marcroft, David Gallay, J. Tynan Burke, L'Erin Ogle, and Douglas Anstruther.

www.ingramcontent.com/pod-product-compliance
Lightning Source LLC
Chambersburg PA
CBHW020623110726
47899CB00002B/622